CW00351421

The door opene ... They saw the outli ... ness of the candles ... several of the men g ...

She was clad in a g ... black, with red flounces, but what had shocked them was the fact that her head and shoulders were completely covered by a black hood like an executioner's, through the slits of which her eyes gleamed and a red mouth partly showed. They could see nothing that would give them a clue as to her age, her looks, her identity. All the womanly tell-tales—colour of hair, texture of skin, firmness of rounded arms—all were hidden. She stood for a long moment, her head moving slightly as her gaze went from one to another, as if checking on them. Then she spoke, in a voice low-pitched, clear and strong.

'Good evening, gentlemen. Welcome to Hell! I am Madam Satan.'

Evelyn Stewart Armstrong was educated in Bath. In 1941 she joined the BBC Engineering Division and worked at Bush House, London on technical control of the European Services, handling news broadcasts and code messages. In 1946 she went to British European Airways as an air stewardess and flew until 1951, when she married Charles Armstrong, a customs officer.

They moved to a village above the Romney Marsh, where Evelyn began to write novels. Five years ago they retired to the south of Spain, where they bought and renovated an old Andalucian farmhouse. She now does her writing at a window overlooking cork woods and the peaks of the Sierra Blanquilla. *Madam Satan* is her first novel to be published as a Masquerade Historical Romance.

MADAM SATAN

EVELYN STEWART ARMSTRONG

MILLS & BOON LIMITED
15–16 BROOK'S MEWS
LONDON W1A 1DR

First published in Great Britain 1985 by Mills & Boon Limited

© Evelyn Stewart Armstrong 1985

Australian copyright 1985 Philippine copyright 1986 This edition 1986

ISBN 0 263 75325 5

Set in 10 on 12 pt Linotron Times 04—0286—60,200

Photoset by Rowland Phototypesetting Limited Bury St Edmunds, Suffolk Made and printed in Great Britain by Cox & Wyman Limited, Reading

To my dear brother
GEOFF
for his love and help in research.

PROLOGUE

THE MEN stood around in the small ante-room, talking to each other, interested, expectant. They had all come in response to the same invitation, and did not quite know what to make of it. Some of them were young, some not so young, but they had one thing in common—their dress, the elegant full-skirted coats, heavily embroidered waistcoats, well-cut knee breeches, and the glitter of shoe-buckles and gleam of seal-fobs, proclaimed them all to be bucks and dandies, the cream of society. They were fashionable, dissipated and rich, and the strange invitation had hinted at a novelty that might please their jaded pleasure-loving appetites.

They had been admitted to the eminently respectable house by a servant—an odd-looking fellow, they had thought—small, lean and brown, clad in sombre black with the exception of a scarlet waistcoat; and now they were in this room, which though tastefully furnished, gave them not a single clue. On one side was the door by which they had entered, on another, a second door on which the servant now knocked twice.

Their conversation ceased, and they all waited. The door opened. A figure came forward, and at the sight an involuntary gasp rose from the group of men.

A woman stood before them, dressed in a black gown trimmed with flounces of rich red. The skirt of the gown was fashionably full, but the close-fitting bodice defined a figure slim yet delightfully rounded, and probably young. Her age, her looks, remained a matter for conjecture, for her head and shoulders were completely covered by a black hood resembling nothing less than the headgear of a public executioner.

The men, taken completely by surprise, stood and stared. Her throat, that tell-tale of age in a woman, might be wrinkled or unlined; her skin might be sallow or fair, clear or pock-marked; her hair could be any colour; even her eyes were only a glitter through the eye-slits, her mouth just visible but its shape unknown. Her arms, which might have given some clue, were covered in long sleeves, with ruffles drooping over the hands. She was unrecognisable, mysterious, macabre.

Then she spoke, in a voice some thought unnaturally deep, but which all later agreed had an accent pure and cultured.

'Good evening, gentlemen. Welcome to Hell! I am Madam Satan . . .'

It all started years ago, she thought, when I defied my father for the first time.

CHAPTER ONE

KATHARINE WALCOTTE stood before the altar in the little country church, and listened to the words of the marriage service. Quite soon now they would reach the point where the wedding would be irrevocable.

She had not looked at Sir Richard since she took her place beside him, but she knew what expression would be in his eyes. Behind her, her father would appear self-satisfied, complacent, hiding the fact that he would be glad when the service was over and he could get back home to enjoy the food and drink of the wedding breakfast and the congratulations of his relatives. Constance Stukely, her bridesmaid and Sir Richard's niece, would be showing a solemn face and concealing her envy that Katharine and not she should be a bride. Then there were Sir Richard's relations—a fair crowd of people, hardly any of whom Katharine had met before. On her side of the aisle the representatives were few; her father's two sisters and their families, and a couple of her mother's cousins by a third or fourth remove.

But the little church was full. Here in this corner of England's West Country, from smiling farmlands heavy with ripening corn, the tenants had turned out in force to witness the wedding of the squire's daughter. That they had come more from curiosity than affection

Katharine did not doubt. Well, they would have a day to remember.

It was high summer, but within the thick stone walls of the church everything was cool, so cool that the perspiration was clammy-cold on Katharine's back and she had to steel herself to repress a shiver. Or was it not entirely the cold, but a touch of nerves? No, why should she be nervous, when over the past few weeks she had rehearsed herself time and time again? Not long now . . . Her mouth was terribly dry, and when she swallowed it felt as if the sides of her throat were sticking together. Was it the Devil that had prompted her to this, or the Lord? Was it any use praying to either of them for strength, and if so, which? It still wasn't too late to change her mind—would it be weakness or just good sense to do so? No, it would soon be over; the words were coming now. She would go through with it.

'Do you, Katharine Louisa, take this man . . .'

. . . She had always hated the name Louisa, but it had been her father's choice, and there could be no argument with that.

Parson Weldon had stopped speaking, and was waiting for her reply. The church was silent, hardly a rustle or a whisper anywhere. She lifted her head sharply, took a deep breath and said, loud enough to hear,

'No! He is my father's choice, not mine. I will not marry him!'

She turned swiftly, and picking up her long skirts she pushed past Constance, whose mouth was just beginning to fall open in an incredulous 'Oh', past her father, whose look was of blank incomprehension, and ran down the aisle between a blur of startled faces, through the open door and out into the churchyard. She fled headlong between the green grass and grey gravestones, hoping desperately that her father would try to save his face by saying a few words to the congregation and thus give her a head start.

On she ran, and almost threw herself under the hoofs of a horse which was just passing the lych-gate as she came through it. She managed to check by clutching the post, and the rider reined in. He looked down at her, and she was aware of dark eyes in a lean brown face, and a mouth on which anger changed to a cynical smile as he asked,

'What in hell do you think you are doing?'

For a split second the thought came to her; if a man like you had been waiting in the church for me, I, knowing nothing of you, might still think marriage worth the gamble. But this was no moment for such foolish speculations. She looked up at him defiantly and retorted,

'Refusing to get married, of course!'

And then, wasting no more time, she picked up her trailing skirts, clambered into the driving-seat of the open carriage—which had brought her to the church and now waited unattended for the return of the bridal couple—slapped the reins and began to drive off.

The man turned in his saddle to look after her, and smiled more broadly at the sight of the beribboned carriage and the girl in dishevelled wedding finery. *Pink*—with that chestnut hair? The rich tresses hung long and loose about her shoulders, a symbol of virginity —deserved? he wondered—and the chaplet of fresh rosebuds which crowned them was sitting somewhat askew. As he watched, he saw a hand come up, pull it off, and toss it into the hedge.

The next moment disaster struck. The girl had been in

too much of a hurry; the horses were unsettled, and fought against her control; the carriage swayed, a wheel slipped and slithered and dropped into the ditch. The carriage, falling at a sharp angle, was saved from overturning only by the strong thick hedge. The girl was now trying to scramble out.

There was a murmuring in the church, and it was growing louder. Doubtless the girl had thrown everything into total confusion. Suddenly curious, the rider cantered up to her, held out his arms, picked her out of the teetering carriage and set her before him.

'This way?' he said, nodding up the road.

'Yes.' And then, belatedly, 'If you please.'

What a crazy situation, he thought. At best I am probably only delaying the affair. 'If you're fleeing from the altar,' he said drily, 'where are you going?'

She looked at him in surprise, as if she hadn't thought of that, and then her mouth set with an obstinate firmness.

'Home. To Walcotte.'

'And then, presumably, you will get over your nerves and marry according to plan.'

'No!' she said sharply. 'I won't. How can my father press it when everyone has heard me refuse?'

'Let us hope you are right.'

It amused him that she showed no embarrassment either at being caught in flight or at being in a stranger's arms on the back of his horse, jolting against his chest, with her head at his shoulder, his face only inches from hers. Now he saw her look become apprehensive.

'I hadn't thought—perhaps he won't care—as long as I marry. Then what *can* I do?'

'Resign yourself to the inevitable?' he suggested cynically.

'*No!* I'll run away! But I can't go now—not like this . . .'

'You would be rather conspicuous—and ill prepared.'

'It would have to be soon—tonight.' She was speaking her thoughts out loud. 'And I must get as far away as possible before he knows I've gone.'

'Good tactics.'

He was amused by the strange wilful girl. How could she hope to succeed in this ridiculous plan? She would be caught at once.

'Which way now?'

'Left at the crossroads.'

'You'll not succeed, you know. You will be caught.'

'Not if I can get to a town.'

'*On foot?* Have you any idea how far . . .?'

'I may meet a carrier who does not know me.'

He looked down at her face, and saw the stubborn set of her mouth. She had spirit; perhaps she deserved a little help.

'I am going visiting this evening,' he said, following his impulse. 'I shall undoubtedly be late. I shall be returning by the Shepton Mallet crossroads—you know them?'

'Yes.'

'If you are there when I pass—about two in the morning, I hazard—I shall take you a few miles along the way.'

'Will you? Oh, thank you. You are very kind. Here is the house.'

An old manor lay back from the road at the end of a drive. It was distinctly run down, he thought, the grounds neglected. As he trotted to the front door he heard the sound of hoofs; a horseman had just turned in from the crossroads.

'It's Father!' she said breathlessly as he lifted her down. 'Thank you.'

She ran up the steps and through the front door. He could see a single rider, a thickset middle-aged figure, urging his horse along the road and nearing the drive. Having assisted the girl, the rider thought it wiser to avoid a confrontation with a furious father. He turned his horse, cantered across the grass of the neglected garden, jumped the rail-fence and gained the road. While the pursuer went up the drive at a gallop, he rode back swiftly the way he had come. Now it is up to her to sort out her problems, he thought. No doubt she will be talked out of her nonsense.

Henry Breedon, Viscount Stonebridge, left for his evening engagement in a distinctly bad temper. Once more his parents had been badgering him on a subject close to their hearts but far from his, a matter which he considered entirely his own business. He could not allow that his father had any cause for complaint. Regret, perhaps, but complaint, no. So he would go his own way.

Earlier he had been somewhat diverted by the incident of—as he called it—the reluctant bride. Now he regretted having given her even such a vague suggestion of assistance in her hare-brained scheme to run away from home. It was quite ridiculous to become involved, when all the rights were on the side of the father. Still, honour compelled him to stand by what he had said. He would take his own time, but when he reached the Shepton Mallet crossroads on his way back to Ember-combe he would stop and see if the girl was waiting there.

He spent a convivial evening, which wiped out his earlier annoyance; he stayed late, and mellowed with wine and agreeable company, set off home. Sometimes on a late night excursion he would take his two-wheeler rather than go on horseback, so the fact that he had done so tonight was unremarkable. But it meant that there was a seat for the girl, if she materialised.

He reined the horse in at the crossroads and looked about him. A half-moon rode now; the hedges were tall and the roadside in shadow. There was no movement except for his horse shifting and tossing its head; no sound save the jingle of harness and the cry of a dog-fox away in the distance. He was about to drive on, when his eyes, becoming accustomed to the shadows, saw what he at first thought was a dark bundle against the trunk of a roadside elm. He got down and went across to it. There was a bundle lying almost in the ditch—but what he had seen was its owner, a woman huddled face downwards where she had fallen.

He turned her over; the faint moonlight showed her face just enough for him to recognise the girl who had fled from the church. Silly creature, he thought—she had been traipsing about the byways at dead of night and had been attacked—what else could she expect? She was alive—he had seen enough dead bodies in his career as a naval officer to tell at once that life was present—but how bad was her case? He lifted her with an arm under her shoulders, and as he did so her head moved and her eyes opened. He felt in his coat pocket, brought out a silver flask, uncapped it and put it to her lips.

'Come, drink a little,' he said.

Obediently she did so; gasped, coughed, caught her breath, and seemed to revive somewhat.

'What happened?' he asked. 'Were you attacked?'

Her mouth twisted—you could not call it a smile.

'Only by my father,' she whispered. 'He beat me.'

A father's privilege, he thought; nevertheless . . .

'Come. Let me help you into the carriage.'

She could hardly walk, and he had almost to lift her into the seat. He was about to get up beside her when she said, 'My bundle—I must have it!'

'Very well.'

He picked it up from the grass, put it behind her, and mounted.

'And then what happened?' he asked.

'He locked me in. He said I'd have nothing but a crust of bread and some water until I agreed . . .' The voice, little more than a whisper, faded away.

'But you got out. How?'

'The only way. I cut up the sheets to make a rope . . .'

'Oh, the time-honoured escape!'

Her eyelids flicked up and a note of defiance came into her voice. 'There was no other! And it wasn't easy—I've never climbed down a rope before. Then I had to walk . . .'

A long, long walk, he now realised. How many miles? Far enough for a fit person by daylight, but for one who had suffered a beating, unable to see the way before moonrise, it must have taken a lot of determination.

He slapped the reins and the horse began to draw the light two-wheeler along the rutted road.

'So what am I to do with you?'

'Please, take me as far as you can. Then I'll go on walking.'

'In your state? And hungry, too? When did you eat?'

'At breakfast. Not much then.'

He drove on, considering the matter. What had he landed himself into? He couldn't abandon the girl. To stop at a cottage and put her into the care of some countrywoman would rouse a lot of unsavoury gossip.

His reputation could look after itself; not so hers. Besides which, it would lead to immediate discovery by her father, and he did not relish the thought of her returning to a man who could beat her and starve her into submission. He had seen her wince, heard her stifle a cry when her back touched the corner of the seat.

'How did he beat you?'

'With his riding-whip.'

That was enough; having befriended the girl, he could not abandon her now.

'There's only one thing for it,' he said. 'You will have to come home with me.'

'No—I can't!'

She shook her head in protest, but he went on.

'Don't worry—you'll be safe enough, and uncompromised. I shall put you in the care of the housekeeper. Now, rest against me. We've some way to go.'

It had all been a nightmare. Katharine was barely conscious as the carriage rattled over the cobbles of a stableyard, stopped, and the driver lifted her down. She allowed herself to be propelled through a door, along a passage, into a room, and placed in a chair.

A little while later she heard the man say, 'I am sorry to disturb you, Mrs Wherry. The girl is in bad case. If you would make her comfortable in one of the guest-rooms, and give her something to eat or drink . . . she is exhausted.'

She went where she was taken, up stairs, along corridors—they seemed to go on for ever—allowed herself to be attended, ate a bowl of bread and milk, and finally fell asleep in a bed of incredible softness. It was like being in heaven after hell.

It was mid-morning when she woke, for the sun was

high and streaming through a window at which a maid
stood, drawing back the curtains. The room was luxurious. The feather mattress on which she lay was thick
and soft, the bedcurtains were a pale shade of fine green
silk damask which also upholstered the dressing stool
and bedside chair, and hung at the windows. Their
colour was echoed in the rugs on the polished floor; by
the fireplace was an armchair covered in creamy yellow
corded silk, and the same yellow covered the cushions in
the window seat. Katharine was struck by the grace and
elegance of the room. The walls were papered with a
pattern of flowers, the ceiling bore a design of plaster-
work motifs and scrolls, and the walnut furniture was
light and quite unlike the solid oak pieces in her home.

The maid set pillows behind her, brought over a tray,
and placed it on the bed.

'Your breakfast, miss.'

She was polite, but her eyes were curious. Katharine
did not dare to ask where she was: better not to show
ignorance but take what comes, she thought, and see
what happens.

She was up and dressed, waiting for the next move,
when she heard a tap at the door.

'Come in,' she said, looking up expectantly. As she
had hoped, it was the lean dark man, her rescuer of
yesterday.

'I hope you are feeling better. It's high time you gave
me a little information.'

'I am better. What do you want to know?'

'Good. First, who are you?'

'Katharine Walcotte. My father is Sir Joshua
Walcotte, of Walcotte Grange.'

'After I left you, you defied your father, refused
to marry his choice, and he gave you a whipping—is

that right? Had you no one to plead for you? Your mother?'

'My mother died more than two years ago. There was no one.'

'Your intended husband?'

'Sir Richard Stukely.' The name came out with bitter contempt. 'He wouldn't have cared. He wants me, and doesn't mind how he gets me. He's a friend of my father—a hunting, gambling, cock-fighting friend. He believes, like my father, that women must be made to obey men.'

'I see. I must tell you that your father has already started a search for you.'

She tried not to show the fear that gripped her. 'Then I must get as far away as I can, as soon as possible.'

He looked at her silently, shrewdly, then said, 'You had better come downstairs in a little while, and see my parents. I shall speak to them first.'

He left the room before she had a chance to thank him.

In the drawing-room, coffee was being taken and Katharine was being discussed.

'Katharine Walcotte . . . Sir Joshua . . .' the Countess of Embercombe was saying. 'Then her mother must have been Lady Clara, the Earl of Hinton's daughter. I remember now; no one could understand at the time why she married beneath her, though there were a number of theories, of course. We should inform the father of the girl's whereabouts.'

Harry Breedon's brows drew together, his face was dark.

'When he has so ill-used her? No, I would say nothing, and find out her plans before we take any action.'

The Earl, who had been silently listening to the exchange, now gave his opinion.

'You cannot go against the father's rights, if as you say she is obviously under age. He has plans for her marriage, you say? Then she must obey him.'

Breedon turned to his mother. 'Mama, I have been away so long, I know none of these people. Who is Sir Richard Stukely? What sort of man, I mean?'

The Countess pursed her lips.

'A man of her father's age, I believe, and hardly a suitable match, from what I have heard. I have not met him, of course. Nevertheless, if it is her father's wish . . .'

'I suppose we had better see the girl,' said the Earl, in some irritation. 'Really, Harry, you do some ill-advised things.'

'Sir, I could hardly leave the girl half-dead by the roadside.'

By now Katharine had discovered that the home of her protector was a place of considerable magnificence; she guessed that it must be Embercombe, which she had heard about but never seen. The fact that he had been referred to as the Viscount Stonebridge confirmed it; so his parents were the Earl and Countess of Embercombe. It was all rather intimidating, and now she was going to have to give them an account of herself.

She felt a qualm of nervousness as she entered the drawing-room. Once inside, there was nothing to put her at her ease. An elderly gentleman in a coat of blue broadcloth with silver buttons, light breeches, silk stockings and silver-buckled shoes looked at her from under a full grey wig with a critical expression whose coldness verged on distaste. Lady Cecily's look was equally unwelcoming, while her son's eyes held only a certain curiosity. Not one of them, Katharine thought, has the faintest idea of what it means to be treated as I have been.

The Earl saw a young girl who stood before them with surprising composure. In her plain dark gown, which hung without hoops in straight folds and was unrelieved save for a white tucker, she looked like a superior kind of servant. But there was no cap on her chestnut hair, and her eyes which were not downcast looked at them with a defiant confidence. But she knew her manners to her elders and superiors; she dropped a small curtsy and waited for them to speak.

'So you are the young lady who does not wish to marry,' the Earl stated coolly.

'I do not wish to marry Richard Stukely,' was the calm reply.

'But your father arranged the marriage. You defied him, and then you ran away.'

'Yes.'

If he had not the wit to understand her reasons, Katharine thought, there was no point in telling him.

'Your father, it seems, is anxious for your return.'

Her heart began to beat faster and she felt a wave of fear pass over her. Surely they would not send her back?

'So that he can force me to marry! I hoped he would not find out where I was—that I would be able to move on somewhere further . . .'

'You realise,' Lord Embercombe commented, 'that wherever you go you can be taken back by force of law.'

'I realise that I am as much his possession as his horses and his dogs. But they are treated rather better—and do not seem to mind how they are mated,' she added, with sudden, savage bitterness.

Lady Cecily gave a gasp of disapproval. Harry Breedon's eyebrows twitched as he suppressed a smile. Lord Embercombe was impassive.

'So, my girl, you are in a difficult position,' he went on.

'Indeed I am, sir. I am most grateful to you for your kindness,' she burst out. 'I can only beg for a little more indulgence.'

'In what respect?'

'Your son, sir, has given me a respite. Now I will make shift for myself, and only ask that someone will put me on the road to a fair-sized town where I could seek employment, and that you do not tell my father my destination.'

'Employment?' interposed Breedon. 'What sort of employment? You are not going to set up as a kitchen-maid, surely?'

She looked at him squarely. 'If necessary, I would do that. But I think I could find myself a post as a governess.'

'A *governess*!' Lady Cecily exclaimed. 'Even if you were capable, you would never obtain a post without references. And those, I imagine, you do not possess.'

'References!' She had not thought of that. They were only for common servants, she believed. 'Then—Then I must take what offers. Any work.'

Lady Cecily gave an impatient move, which set her panniered skirt rustling, and spoke sharply. 'Tush, child, you are talking nonsense! Your mother was nobility, you are gentry and cannot accept common employment. I suppose you have some silly notion of changing your name and becoming a lady's maid or a milliner! It won't work. You would be unprotected, and subjected to a life which would be infinitely worse than marriage to a man you think is not to your liking.'

'Nothing could be worse than that.'

'Fiddlesticks! Hire yourself for employment, and you will soon find yourself forced to give some man every-thing Stukely would claim—and that without benefit of marriage lines. Next would come dismissal, as soon as you were pregnant. Then a bastard child, and, if you were lucky, the poorhouse for the both of you. It happens all the time.'

Katharine felt herself flushing as shame and fury rose within her. 'That is dreadful! I would not let it happen to me.'

'No?' The word was as hard as stone. 'You could not prevent it.'

The Earl's face softened a little, though his wife's did not. 'Child, you do not understand the world,' he said. 'Without a man's protection, a woman cannot govern her life, and there are always unscrupulous men who make women their victims. Be sensible—make the best of the marriage arranged for you.'

It was what her mother had told her years ago, and she still rebelled against it.

'If I am taken back by force, and compelled to marry him, I will have to do so. But I will first try to live my life in my own way.'

Lord and Lady Embercome exchanged resigned glances.

'Is there no one you can go to for the time being?' asked Breedon. 'Some relative or family friend?'

'No,' she said flatly. 'That is, no one who will not feel obliged to tell my father where I am, and send me back.'

'Then it seems there is nothing we can do,' said the Earl. 'But you may stay here until we see what action your father takes. That is all I can promise.'

He nodded to her, and looked away. She was dismissed. She pulled herself up as straight as a ramrod, drew her shawl about her and walked to the door, blinking back the tears of humiliation that began to fill her eyes.

Without apparently hurrying, Harry Breedon was at the door before her. He opened it for her with a little bow, and as he saw her out, he murmured, 'I shall come and speak to you later.'

'What an extraordinary girl,' Lady Cecily commented. 'I do positively regret you involved us in her affairs, Harry.'

Breedon said no more, but went off to his room, where he smoked a pipe of tobacco and considered the situation. Eventually, sending a maid ahead to announce him, he sought out the girl.

Katharine was sitting bolt upright on the window seat, and rose as he came in. He waved her back to her seat and swung a dainty cabriole-legged chair in front of her, straddled it, folded his arms on the back, placed his chin on his arm and surveyed her critically.

'You look a determined young woman. Some would call you obstinate.'

'If it is obstinate to want some say in how I live my life, then, yes, I am.'

'Has your father treated you like this before?' he asked abruptly.

'Has he whipped me? No. But I have never disobeyed him before.'

'Ah. So rebellion is a new thing for you?'

'Yes.'

'And I imagine you now find cause to regret it.'

'No. My resolve is strengthened.'

Breedon gazed at her. Her eyes, he decided, were

hazel, almost green, and fearless. Her features were good, her skin clear and unmarked, her mouth well-shaped and firm. If her expression would soften she would be good looking; some men would find her attractive. She was not his type of woman, of course, nothing like Annabel Harcourt, who was blonde, full-breasted, with dimpled cheeks, plump arms and a languishing way with her which was truly feminine. Reluctantly he dragged his straying mind back to this awkward female.

'And if you don't go back, what will you do?'

'I have told you. I shall find work. I cannot believe that someone will not employ me as a governess without references.'

'And what could you teach children, pray?'

'I could teach history, geography, mathematics, French and, when needed, Latin and Greek.'

He stared at her for a moment, then burst out laughing.

'I am not joking!' she retorted with a hint of annoyance. 'I have been well taught, and I am convinced I could pass on my knowledge.'

'But it's ridiculous!' he exclaimed. 'Why did your father have you educated like that, and then decide to marry you off to a country squire? Did he not intend you to be spouse to a Cabinet Minister, at the very least?'

She was irritated by his facetiousness, but decided she might as well tell him the facts.

'Father did not know what Mr Weldon, our parson, was teaching me. I wanted to learn, for I did not see why boys should be educated and girls kept ignorant. As for . . . Stukely . . .' The name was so distasteful she had difficulty in bringing it out. 'He wants to marry me, and my father is handing me over in return for the cancellation of his gambling debts.'

'*What?*'

'Yes. I am being sold—like a horse or a dog.'

He stared at her in silence.

'You need not look so surprised,' she went on. 'To me, it seems that marriage arrangements mean that the women are invariably sold or bartered. Even if I liked Stukely, I would still find it unpleasant to be treated like a piece of property with a cash value. A woman should have some say in her marriage.'

The girl was appallingly self-opinionated, he thought. No wonder her father had lost his temper, though that did not excuse him.

'So you would alter the system, would you?'

'I think women should have the same right to live their lives that men enjoy, to refuse someone uncongenial, and, if they wish, to take such employment as they care for.'

'Do you, indeed? That would turn society into total chaos. I suppose you would like to see women becoming soldiers, sailors, blacksmiths and builders, lawyers and surgeons?'

There was a studied irony in his voice. She tried not to let it irritate her further.

'I would not wish to take things to extremes; there are some occupations for which we are not fitted. I do not think to be soldiers or sailors, or blacksmiths or builders, would be suitable. But I do not see why an intelligent woman should not be a lawyer, or a surgeon. Women can stand the sight of blood better than men can.'

Breedon bowed his head upon his hands. 'You are a crazy wench,' he said finally. 'But it is useless to discuss your lunatic notions. What are we to do with you, that is the question? You had better think of a sensible suggestion in short order, for your father will soon compel us by law to give you up! Damme, why won't you marry Stukely!'

She gave him a withering look in which contempt and anger strove together.

'Spoken like a man!' she cried. 'So I am to give my life over to that horrible creature to pay my father's debts and to save you a little trouble! I think I had better leave now and start walking. I'd rather die in a ditch than go back to that.'

As she rose to her feet, Breedon stretched out a hand and caught her wrist. 'It's as bad as that, is it? I said what I did because marriage is the only way in which you can escape from your father, and since you are no doubt under age you can marry only with his permission. How old are you, by the way?'

She looked down at him and did not try to release herself. 'Just seventeen.'

And Stukely was an old lecher in his fifties, Breedon had heard. It was not a pretty picture when one gazed on it. But what was the alternative? Either she would be caught and taken back, or, unprotected, she would he seduced and abandoned. No, with her principles, it would be rape. His mouth twisted. She was destined for that, it seemed—in or out of marriage. He dropped her wrist, cursing himself for becoming involved. Why couldn't he just turn her out of doors to fend for herself? She was not his responsibility.

She turned away. Her figure outlined against the light from the window was slim and shapely, the arms slender, her neck a delicate column, her hair tawny and beautiful. He tried to see her face—was she struggling not to cry? And was there nothing he could do?

Suddenly an idea flashed into his head—an idea so

foolish, so outrageous, that he thrust it from him, yet it returned at once, bringing with it a train of thought which made the whole thing appear simple and brilliant, and almost possible . . . No, she would not do it. One could not expect her to, yet . . .

'You heard what my mother said,' he began. 'She was right. You could not survive, trying to make your own way, without help or protection.'

'I could try. And I'd rather—'

'—die in a ditch. I know. Don't argue, just listen to me and answer my questions. You say you won't marry Stukely—but would you marry anyone else?'

'Father would not let me marry anyone else,' she said, as if explaining to a child.

'Damme, woman, answer me! Are you totally opposed to marriage?'

'I think . . . perhaps not . . . But there is no one . . .'

'Very well. Then you had better marry me.'

'*You?*'

'Yes. Oh, I am not going to be idealistic about it. I am not offering you my name, my protection and a life of comfort for nothing, just because I am sorry for you and you will not be actually repulsive when viewed across the dining-table. I am not that sort of fool. I shall want something in return.'

She sat down suddenly on the window seat, passed her tongue over her lips and then asked in a voice that was almost a whisper, 'And what—what would that be?'

'An heir.'

Her bones seemed to turn to water as his dark eyes looked coolly into hers. He repeated the words.

'Yes, An heir.'

CHAPTER
TWO

KATHARINE GAZED at Breedon with an amazement that verged on incomprehension. How could he make such a proposal?

'Don't look so surprised,' Breedon continued easily. 'That is the reason most men marry—pleasure can be had without it. But I suppose you are entitled to an explanation. The situation is this.'

He paused, and looked wryly at her before continuing.

'I am my father's only son. I should not have been the heir, but my elder brother, still a bachelor, was killed a year ago in a riding accident. He had always said he had plenty of time to marry—it was ironical that he had none. As for me, the woman I wanted to marry was already the wife of another man. My father considers preference irrelevant where the matter of succession is concerned. He is continually pressing me to marry and have a son so that he can see his title reasonably safe from extinction. When I say "continually", I mean every time I am on leave—for I am a serving naval officer —and repeatedly in his letters. It is a great bore and a nuisance to me. If I agreed to my father arranging a marriage, it would be a conventional affair, and I do not intend to give up the service and dance attendance on a wife. If *we* married, we would have the understanding that, once you had given me a son, I would ask nothing more of you—nor you of me.'

'And your parents? What would they say?' she gasped.

'Of course they would not know of the arrangement. But they would be freed from the apprehension that I might be killed before there was another generation to inherit. We would each go our own way: myself on active service and to spend my leaves how and where I choose, and you to make your own social life, being your own mistress. It seems to me it would be a perfectly good arrangement, but plainly you will wish to consider it. I shall come back in an hour or so for your decision.'

Without more ado he left her.

Katharine sat in the window seat as if stunned. Marriage to a man other than Stukely was the one thing she had never considered. But *this*! A completely cold-blooded arrangement, in which they would be husband and wife until she had produced a son, was another matter. She could not possibly do that.

And yet—the alternative seemed to be marriage to Stukely, the very thought of which filled her with revulsion. At least, this man was not actually repulsive to her, and had shown himself capable of kindness. And he was in love with someone else—that was an advantage. He would make no more demands on her than were absolutely necessary, he had said that. He was unsympathetic and offhand, but he was not without heart, or he would have left her where she lay on the roadside.

Now that she had got over the shock of his proposal, she began to feel that she could do worse than accept. Nevertheless, as she thought it over, she still considered it totally outrageous. After all, Breedon would be doing very well out of it. He would have a complaisant wife, and complete freedom, with the heir his family obviously so much desired. For him it was an easy solution. But for her? Though his family were immeasurably more wealthy than her father, she would be a wife without a penny to call her own, tied to them by marriage, which meant by convention and financial necessity.

Why must women always be virtual slaves, she thought, striking her hands together in fury at such subjection. And why did all women but herself seem to accept it, even to like a life of subservience and acquiescence to a dominant male? The whole tribe of womankind was passively spending its time in making the best of a life of servitude. It was too much to hope that she could achieve anything different. Nevertheless her mind continued to turn the matter over, although she told herself that nothing could possibly come of it.

An hour or so later Betty came in with a tray of coffee, laid with two cups. Breedon was immediately behind her.

'I hope you will allow me to take coffee with you, Miss Walcotte?' he said blandly.

'Certainly, Lord Stonebridge,' she repeated, and busied herself in pouring out to his taste, whereafter they sat for a minute, sipping in silence.

'Well, have you made up your mind?' he demanded.

'I do not think,' she said precisely, 'that you realise that your suggestion is quite impossible. My father would never agree to let me marry you. He has promised me to Stukely, who is his friend; and he would force me to marry him now, to punish me for my disobedience.'

'I know that,' Breedon retorted. 'But, assuming that we *could* marry—would you agree to do so?'

She took another sip of coffee.

'I would consider it—subject to a certain condition.'

He stared at her, then gave a short laugh. 'You never cease to amaze me! I am making you an offer, and you start setting conditions! What may it be, pray?'

'It occurs to me that the arrangement would be one-sided, with you having all the advantages.'

'*All!* You seem to forget that you would be gaining an establishment and a position far above anything to which you have any right to aspire. You would live a life of luxury, you would be totally free to follow your own amusements . . .'

'Free! Free within the bounds of an apparently conventional marriage, which to me is not freedom. I should be dependent on your family for everything.'

'I can quite see that to your untrammelled spirit that would be restriction indeed,' he retorted sarcastically. 'But you would not find us ungenerous.'

'You forget that you are asking me to give you what your father most desires—and that you cannot get it except by marriage. I have been thinking it over, and I am aware if you contracted a marriage arranged in the normal way, you would not be able to be so dismissive of your wife as you would be to me. You admitted that. Any other marriage would be most irksome—that is why you have not married before.'

'How perceptive of you.'

'So, if I were to marry you and give you the son you desire, I consider that I should be compensated for my trouble. I would do it, if you would guarantee on the child's birth to pay me quite a large sum of money—and to arrange it so that the money is *mine*, outright; for I know, you see, that a wife's money belongs to her husband.'

'Whatever next! So I am to *pay* you for having the child! Isn't keeping you in luxury for life enough?'

'You would do that in any case, for any wife. Don't you understand—I want some money that is *mine*, which I can use exactly how I please, and over which I would have sole control. I don't think that is asking too much, when you would be having everything else your own way.'

'And how much had you in mind?' The tone of his voice was even more sarcastic.

'I haven't decided. We could settle that between us.'

'It is an interesting suggestion, but I am afraid I do not follow your logic. You object to being forced to marry Stukely, because you consider your father is selling you like a chattel. Now you are proposing to sell yourself to me—like a whore.'

She flinched as if he had struck her, and her eyes blazed at him.

'That is not so! I know very little of such matters, but a whore, I believe, sells herself repeatedly to any man who wants her by reason of his lust. You do not lust for me, you have made that plain, and I would not go to any other man, from inclination or for money. I am asking only for some financial independence in return for giving you what you want—a matter which I expect to find both hard and distasteful.'

The colour rose in her cheeks and her voice trembled a little as she went on, but her words were firm and clear.

'I shall be quite at your mercy, for I—have never —have never—*known* a man. But call me a whore once more, and there will be no more talk of a marriage.

He put down his cup and made a swift gesture towards her.

'I apologise. It was a cruel thing to say to you, and I did so unthinkingly. I accept your condition. *Now* will you marry me?'

There was a long pause.

'Yes, if it can be managed.'

His hand went out and closed over hers. In his strong warm grasp her fingers were slim and cool. She let her hand lie in his for a moment before withdrawing it.

'Then it's a bargain,' he said.

'I agree. But how can we marry?'

'It is quite simple. As you say, since you are a minor you cannot marry without your father's consent. That is English law.'

'Yes.'

'But it is not Scottish law. Have you not heard of Gretna Green?'

'Gretna Green . . .?' The words came out slowly, thoughtfully. 'That is in Scotland?'

'Just over the border. Since the law on clandestine marriages was passed a few years ago—in 1754, or thereabouts—headstrong young misses who wish to marry a man not of their parents' choice have been eloping to get married by Scottish law, which permits it over the age of sixteen without parental consent, and is an extraordinarily simple business. And England has to recognise it.'

'And you suggest we do that?'

'Yes. It would be an amusing escapade, and would thoroughly spike your father's guns. Now, I think it is time you told me something about yourself. Have you always been at loggerheads with him?'

'He has always hated me, because I wasn't a boy. And he was cruel to my mother—because though she had other babies, they all died. She wasn't strong. Then she died. So he has no heir, and he hated us both for it.'

'But your mother was kind to you?'

'She loved me!' Her words were swift and defensive.

'She did all she could for me, but there's not much you can do against a man like Father. If it hadn't been for her, I'd have had no schooling—nothing.'

'And after she died?'

'He dismissed Mrs Partridge, our housekeeper—she was good to me, and told me how to keep house. But he hadn't realised I'd grown up. Stukely did . . . and . . .'

Katharine faltered. The memory was fresh and distasteful.

'Stukely took a fancy to you, I suppose?'

'Yes. He often tried to kiss me—to put his hands over me—I couldn't always avoid him . . .'

Breedon's eyes hardened.

'And so a marriage was arranged—in settlement of gambling debts, you said?'

'Yes. I was told one day, and the next day he came with Mrs Cusson—she goes hunting with them—and they took me to Devizes and bought me a wedding dress.'

She pushed out of her mind the memory of the drive back in the coach with Mrs Cusson. Stukely rode alongside the carriage, while inside Maria Cusson probed her innocence and enlightened her in coarse terms about the facts of married life, the ritual of the bride-bed, and of what a husband might expect of a wife. It had sickened her, and it still did. It would be a revolting experience, but at least this man was not repulsive to her, as Stukely was. Since she could not escape, she must take the better bargain.

Breedon was looking at her closely. She brought her attention back to what he was saying.

'I see. Well, this marriage will be a hurried business, too. We shall say nothing to my parents—best not to involve them in the plot. I'll order the coach to leave

after dark, so be ready. We'll be as secret as possible, so
that gossip will take a little while to reach your father.
The turnpike road is good, we can make some distance
in the dark, and we should have sufficient start so that
even if he guesses our intentions he'll not catch us this
side of the border.'

And so, in Breedon's travelling coach with its coat of
arms on the door panel, they went to Gretna Green.
They bought a wedding ring on the way; they were
married over the anvil in the smithy; and returned, in
more leisurely stages than they had gone, to Embercombe, to whatever reception might await them.

They had reached Embercombe lodge. The great iron
gates between twin stone pillars, each surmounted by an
heraldic beast holding a shield, were swung open for the
travelling coach, and they continued on up the drive.
Katharine remembered seeing those entrance gates in
passing a few years ago; now she was to have her first
sight of Embercombe, for she had been unconscious on
entering the house, and they had left it in the dark. A
feeling of nervous excitement began to creep over her.
She leaned forward, looking out of the window.

They swung round a bend in the tree-lined avenue,
and the prospect suddenly opened out to show her
Embercombe in all its magnificence. A main block with
a central flight of shallow entrance steps, rows of windows on two storeys topped by a series of dormers, a
portico, and a roof surmounted by a cupola was flanked
by wings on either side; it was all grey stone and glass,
harmonious, classical, and most imposing. And it was to
be her home—or rather, one of them.

When they entered the house, the major-domo informed Breedon that the Earl and the Countess were in

the small drawing-room. The entrance hall was vast, and
soared up the height of two storeys, with a staircase
curving up on either side joined by a gallery across the
back. Almost before she had time to look about her,
Breedon led Katharine straight across the hall into a
huge formal saloon behind it, and thence into more
connecting rooms. She could not be sure if she had seen
these rooms before or not; Embercombe seemed to
consist of so many rooms, all elegantly decorated with
brocades and mirrors, paintings and glass, so that as yet
she could not distinguish one from another.

The Earl and his wife struggled not to express surprise
when their son entered.

'Harry!' his mother exclaimed at last. 'Where have
you been?'

Then her eyes fell on Katharine.

'You have brought her back! Kindly explain yourself.'

'I could hardly leave her behind, Mama. We have
been to Gretna Green. We are married.'

At this abrupt statement Lady Cecily fell back in her
chair, groped in her pocket and brought out a gold
smelling-bottle. In silence she opened it and sniffed at it,
and though Katharine privately felt the Countess was in
no danger of fainting, being made of sterner stuff, she
took some while fanning her face with her lace handkerchief and shook her head several times. Lord
Embercombe's jaw had dropped, and his eyes, usually
languidly hooded, opened wide; then he collected
himself and was the first to speak.

'You young jackanapes! You are not serious?'

'Never more so, sir. It seemed the best solution to all
our problems.'

'Solution! *Solution!* You have made a damn sight
more of them!'

Breedon set a chair for Katharine and then took one himself. Stretching his legs comfortably before him he responded, 'Come, sir. I truly think we have solved two, and made no more.'

'Do you mean to tell me—' Lady Cecily's voice was cold and terrible '—that you *eloped*? That you are married to this—this *nobody*?'

'An earl's granddaughter, Mama.'

'On her mother's side! A nobody now! And with that monstrous father!'

The Earl added his protest.'Christ Almighty, Harry, there was no need for you to do it!'

'Papa, that is most unreasonable. You have continually urged me to marry.'

His mother's voice came out like a gust of despair. 'We did not intend you to marry the daughter of a small squire! Your father was ready to arrange a proper match . . .'

The Earl took her up. 'You know damn well I had my eye on . . . Oh, never mind, it's too late now. You've burned your boats and saddled yourself with a load of mischief. That is, if it's true. You're not joking?'

'I was never more serious.'

Lord Embercombe lifted the quizzing-glass which hung from his watch-chain, and raising it to his eye, looked Katharine up and down, slowly and exhaustively.

'You've done this without consideration. Much better have let me choose you a wife. You don't have to marry a girl because you want to bed her! What I want to know is, will she be a good breeder? Her mother wasn't.'

Katharine stiffened with shock and disgust. He was no better than her father in his attitude to women. And he had not finished.

'She looks too thin to me. Can't imagine why you wanted her. Not at all the type you've favoured in the past. And you haven't much time either—your leave lasts only another couple of months or so. If she's slow in coming to the point . . .'

'That is all *my* concern, Papa. You are embarrassing Kate—and quite unnecessarily, I assure you. Now, if you will forgive us, we would like to refresh ourselves. It has been a long and tiring journey.'

He stood up and offered Katharine his arm. She had not said a word during the whole interview. She had not been addressed, nor was she expected to offer any comment or opinion on a matter which concerned her so closely. Plainly, that was how things were expected to be. She was now an object to be used in the furtherance of their dynastic plans, since they could not get rid of her for a better; and she had exchanged one servitude for another, considerably more luxurious, but basically the same.

The news quickly spread that Breedon and Katharine had returned, and Sir Joshua appeared soon enough.

The interview that followed between Sir Joshua and Breedon, at which Katharine was present, was brief —thanks to Breedon—but long enough for her father to tell her what he thought of her. When he was forced to accept the fact that she and Breedon were married and his plans totally upset, he turned on her, and Breedon could see him for what he was.

'You—You Satan's bitch!' he shouted. 'I might have known you'd turn out badly! So Stukely wasn't good enough for you, but the first fancy fellow who puts a hand up your skirt makes you so hot that you let him mount you! *Marriage!* You're both trying to put a good face on it! *You*—the shy, stand-offish maid who didn't even want a kiss from my friend Stukely! Just a hot little whore after all! Well, I've finished with you—you'll get nothing from me. Nothing, I tell you, now or when I die! So make the best of what he chooses to give you before he tires of you—you whoring slut of a she-devil!'

Katharine stood, trembling with horror, rage and disgust, and gritted her teeth. If she spoke, it would only add fuel to the flames of her father's wrath, and the scene would be prolonged and even worse.

'I trust you have now had your say,' Breedon commented. 'I must ask you to leave us. Your presence is unwelcome to me and distressing to my wife, and your remarks are as offensive as you yourself are in person. Good day.'

Well, you could say that was one hurdle over, thought Katharine. I need never see him again.

But there was still another ordeal to go through. Breedon had not yet taken the rights of a husband. He had been considerate and forbearing on the journey from Gretna Green; on the first night that they shared a room, and were plainly to share a bed, he had caught her look of apprehension.

'God Almighty, child!' he had exclaimed. 'You don't think I am going to insist on initiating you into your marital duties tonight? You're hardly used to me—I am not so much of a brute!'

And he had left her, to take a drink in the inn parlour while she went to bed. He had not yet insisted; but he must do so soon. That was part of the bargain. She could not forget the disgusting, frightening description Maria Cusson had given her to prepare her for marrying Stukely, try as she might to ignore it until the time came.

The next few weeks at Embercombe were challenging

and not altogether enjoyable. Lady Cecily had determined that since she could not get rid of Katharine, she
would do her best to mould her into the semblance of a
suitable wife for Viscount Stonebridge. She began to
tutor the girl, morning, noon and night. Etiquette;
precedence; manners; dress; everything was dealt with
exhaustively, even the business of making tea, serving
coffee and using a fan. Everything was important;
nothing was too trivial.

Lady Cecily was in half-mourning, so a few of her
older light-coloured gowns were made over for
Katharine while a mantua-maker was summoned to
Embercombe to bring materials and fashion-plates for a
choice of new garments. Katharine—who had little say
in the choice—was horrified at the enormous amount of
clothes that were ordered for her, and furious when she
heard Lady Cecily say imperiously to the fitter,

'You will of course arrange that the gowns can be let
out. It may soon be necessary.'

It was obvious why; she expects to control everything,
thought Katharine grimly.

Breedon went out riding a great deal—in the morning
to set him up for the day—for the rest, Katharine did not
know whether he went abroad for business or pleasure.
She made a point of being in the breakfast-room when
he returned from his first ride. It was the only time she
could be sure of seeing him alone. Now she was envying
Breedon his freedom and outdoor exercise, and thought
there was no harm in telling him so.

'You ride every morning,' she said. 'How I wish I
could join you sometimes.'

He looked up from his plate with an expression of
surprise. 'You ride? I did not think that such a frivolous
pursuit would interest you.'

'I don't ride very well,' she admitted. 'But I enjoy it. I had to learn on the sly, from one of the grooms.'

He made a wry face. 'Grooms are not normally the best teachers, but you can come out with me one morning, if you wish, and I'll see how you do.'

She twisted her napkin in her hands. 'I—I have no habit. Many gowns have been ordered, but nothing for riding.'

Pursing his lips, he commented, 'Ah. I dare say Mama has her reasons for that. We shall make our own arrangements. By the way, it is high time you began to use my name. You avoid it as if it were some new heresy. So, come now, say to me, "Harry, I shall be pleased to accompany you to the habit-maker".'

She gave him a radiant smile, and repeated his words.

'There, it was simple. Would this afternoon suit you, Kate?'

'It would suit me very well, Harry.'

'Excellent, Kate. Pray pour me some more coffee.'

That evening Breedon did not go out after supper, so the family of four sat together in the drawing-room, the men sipping their brandy, Lady Cecily stitching at some embroidery, while Katharine began to dip into a book she had found that evening in the library.

The Earl shifted irritably in his chair. 'Why are we sitting here like a set of stuffed dummies?' he asked. 'There are four of us. Let us take a hand of whist.'

There was a long pause while Lady Cecily wrestled with her thoughts. Then she lodged her needle in her work.

'Harry, you may ring for James to set out the table.'

Katharine felt nervousness mounting within her as a gaming-table was opened and cards set forth.

'Your father and I will play against you and Katharine, Harry,' the Countess said.

Katharine forced out her confession. 'I am sorry, Lady Cecily. I must admit that I do not know how to play.'

Three faces turned to her with expressions of utter astonishment.

'You do not *know* . . .'

'Damme, child, how could you not . . .'

'You've never played, Kate?' Breedon set a handful of counters in the middle of the table. 'That is indeed a surprise. Well, then, we shall have to teach you.'

'It will be a very poor game,' Lady Cecily snapped. 'We might as well play dummy.'

'She must learn sooner or later, Mama. Better in private than in public, surely?'

'True. Let us hope she is not too long about it.'

Why does she so often speak as if I were not here? Katharine wondered, as they took their places at the table and Breedon began to deal the cards. When the Embercombes saw that she had not the slightest idea of the game, instructions and comments were shot at her from all sides. She became more and more confused. A game of cards was the most trivial thing, she told herself, yet she knew that a great deal of her social poise would ultimately depend on her ability to learn it. In society everyone played whist: to be a poor player was to condemn oneself to be classed as a fool and a liability whenever cards were proposed. At the present moment, to spoil the Embercombes' amusement would make her more unpopular than she already was. Luckily for her, Breedon had the sense to understand the extent of her bewilderment.

'I think it would be better if only one of us instructed

Kate. Let me tell her what to do, and we shall not count
this game towards the rubber.'

To her relief that was agreed, and he went on, 'Now,
Kate, the game depends on taking tricks, the highest
card of each four played, winning. For each trick won, a
counter is taken for scoring—there are thirteen here,
you see, for a game. Now for the rules.'

Game followed game, until they had played three
rubbers.

Towards the end she felt she was getting a grasp of the
play, that if she could only think about it she might be
able to make something of it. She and Breedon had lost
all three rubbers, and the Embercombes, at least,
looked satisfied.

The next day, whenever she had a quiet moment, such
as when sorting Lady Cecily's silks or sitting over her
own embroidery, she thought about whist. The pattern
of it had fallen into shape. In the evening whist was again
proposed. Katharine took her place at the table with a
feeling of some excitement, and when the game began
she set about testing her speculations. She made mis-
takes, of course; at first through inexperience, and later
through over-confidence, though from her deliberately
impassive expression no one could guess which was
which. But she surprised the Embercombes and pleased
Breedon, for they won one rubber out of three; and at
least one gained by Lord Embercombe had been due to
the fact that he and his partner had been extraordinarily
lucky in the deal.

Katharine's habit arrived from Wells, and Breedon
said they would go riding together. He found points to
criticise in her style, but was not too censorious.

'Egad, Kate, you ride better than I dared hope when
you told me you had been taught by a groom,' he said.

'You seem to have a feeling for it—I dare say we shall polish you up into something quite acceptable.'

It was the custom at Embercombe to give a dinner to all the tenants on the occasion of a family event such as a birth, a coming of age, or a marriage. The fact that Breedon and Katharine had not been married at Embercombe with all the customary celebrations could not be allowed to deprive the tenants of a good feed, Harry told her. They would expect it—and it was their opportunity to meet the heir's bride.

'It is all very rustic,' he reassured her. 'Nothing to worry about.'

Nevertheless she knew she would be expected to make a good showing.

The day of the tenants' dinner was fine and sunny. Mrs Wherry, no doubt relieved that the visitors' boots would not be thick with mud, bustled about with cheerful efficiency, seeing that the servants' hall, where it was to be held, was prepared and decorated. Extra tables had been put up and laid with white cloths; down the centre of each was a trail of greenery interspersed with bunches of flowers and ears of wheat; the walls were garlanded; and then the boards were set out with cutlery, plates and tankards. The top table, where Katharine and Breedon were to sit with the highest ranking of the tenants, was furnished with china instead of pewter, and the tankards were supplemented by wine glasses. Then, as the time for the arrival of the guests drew near, the food began to appear. Large crusty loaves of country bread; dishes of home-made butter and slabs of cheese; bowls of pickles; then great rounds of beef, joints of mutton, rabbit pies, bacon and ham; until Katharine, an interested spectator, wondered how the tables could hold the load. And in the larder were puddings, custards, syllabubs and jugs of cream.

She had tried to strike a happy compromise between wearing a gown which was too grand for the occasion and one which by its simplicity would show insufficient respect for the company; the lower orders were notoriously touchy, she had been told by Lady Cecily. Her gown of soft green silk was patterned over with separate little multicoloured sprigs, with a row of small green ribbon bows marching down from neckline to pointed waist, becomingly full-skirted and close-bodied, with a demure lace tucker, and lace frills inside the loose sleeves. For jewellery she wore her mother's coral necklet and earrings, which she had salvaged in her flight from Walcotte, glad that Lady Cecily had not taken it into her head to insist on lending her jewellery or supervising her dress. Perhaps she wanted to see how Katharine would carry off the celebration unaided? When Breedon joined her he made no comment on her appearance, but his eyes held approval, and she began to feel more confident.

The tenants began to arrive, and were greeted. At last all the places save theirs were filled, and Breedon led her to the top table. With a great scraping of chairs and benches everyone stood to toast the pair of them, and then Breedon called out.

'Thank you all! Now set to, everybody! Let's get some food inside us before we start speechmaking!'

There was a general murmur of approval. Plates began to be filled and conversation started, quietly at first, then, as food and drink eased formality, there was a hum and buzz of chatter. Katharine knew only too well that she was the centre of attention, people constantly glancing up from their plates to give her a quizzing look.

It was unnerving; she felt as if every mouthful she took was being watched, and it inhibited her appetite considerably. Breedon was not so troubled. He's used to it, she thought.

The top table was furnished with both beer and wine; she preferred wine, and Breedon filled her glass. With all eyes on her it was easier to drink than to eat, and besides, she had to carry on some conversation as well. She must not appear haughty or reserved. When the edge of the communal appetite was blunted, the leading tenant farmer levered his bulk out of his chair and banged on the table for attention.

'Now, friends, before we get so full of food that we forget what we're here for, I reckon it's time to say a word to our host.'

There was a hum of general approval.

'We all know why we're here,' he went on. 'It's to celebrate a happy occasion—the marriage of our landlord's son—Lord Embercombe's heir, Viscount Stonebridge—though I dare say many of us still think of him as Mr Henry Breedon. It seems he's an impetuous young man—he rushed off and got married without any of us guessing at it, but now we can see why he was in such a hurry! It looks to me as if he's a lucky man.'

A roar of agreement came from the lower tables. Katharine was floating in a kind of euphoric trance; she felt happy, confident, completely unworried, perfectly relaxed. Breedon had kept refilling her glass so that she did not know how much she had drunk, but it did not matter; the wine was rich and smooth and slipped down so easily and pleasantly. Some of the remarks were becoming a little near the knuckle, but one must not be offended; country people were close to nature, and weddings always called forth earthy wit, most of which she didn't understand. Thank heavens she didn't have to make a speech, for she would have no idea what to say.

Horrors! What had Mr Slater just said?

'We haven't heard a word from your lady, my lord. Will she not give us the pleasure of hearing her voice?'

Now the hall was quiet, and Breedon was looking at her with a smile which was intended to be encouraging, yet she could see the doubt in his eyes.

'Must I?' she whispered.

'Just a word,' he murmured back.

She got to her feet, her hands gripping the edge of the table, and took a deep breath. Innumerable pink blobs were lifted up to her—they were faces, looking, waiting. What could she say? It must be simple, for her mind refused to produce a single well-turned phrase.

'My good friends . . .' she began, and there was a burst of clapping. Encouraged, she went on, 'My good friends, I have enjoyed meeting you. I can only hope that I shall not disappoint you—this new life is strange to me, but I shall do my best. Thank you—for giving me—so kind a welcome.'

Her legs were trembling, and she sat down hurriedly.

'Well done,' Breedon murmured under the cheers which followed her words. Thankfully she took a long drink of wine. Now he was on his feet.

'Well, good people, with your permission, my wife and I shall leave you to enjoy the rest of your dinner. Don't stint yourselves, or I shall be offended, for you are here to celebrate! Once again, we thank you for all your good wishes.'

He put his hand beneath her arm and led her out as the tenants, raggedly at first, and then in full voice, gave them a rousing chorus. It must have been reaction that made her feel quite uncertain on her feet, and she was

glad of Breedon's supporting arm. As the door of the
servants' hall closed behind them and the din subsided,
he grinned down at her.

'I don't suppose you want to face Mama and give an
account of yourself, do you?'

'Not if it can be helped,' she answered, returning an
impish smile.

'Neither do I! Let us make an escape and steal upstairs
to our room.'

Still holding her arm, he led her to the back stairs, and
like a pair of conspirators they tiptoed up and then fled
along the corridors until they reached the door of their
bedroom. She still had that pleasant floating sensation,
and hurrying had made her quite out of breath. It was all
delightfully foolish. As he closed the door, she ran to the
bed and plumped down upon it.

Breedon, looking like a naughty boy, flung himself beside her. She lay back and looked at him in
happy amazement, for she had never seen him like this
before.

'Oh, Kate!' he said. 'I like you when you forget to be
solemn and high-minded!'

Now that she was relaxed and lying on the bed, she
began to feel slightly sleepy, and not in the mood to
resent the remark as she might have done.

'I'm not high-minded,' she said drowsily. 'Just afraid
. . . afraid of being . . . what I don't want to be . . .'

She meant, of being her father's daughter, but did not
want to say so.

'If you choose, you can afford to be frivolous sometimes.'

'Would you like me . . . to be frivolous?'

'I should not object.'

She turned her head sideways and smiled at him. 'I

thought it would not be suitable behaviour . . . for a
viscountess . . . which it seems I am, though it's all very
odd . . .'

'Not suitable! You don't know many viscountesses!'

'I don't know any . . . and your mother . . .'

'Bother Mama! She's too formal by half. Do you
know, Kate, you look very pretty today. It's not
surprising the tenants all admired you.'

'*Did* they?' She sat up suddenly in surprise, so suddenly that she felt a trifle dizzy, and lay back again. 'But
you did not.'

He laughed. 'Don't angle for compliments! I told you
you were pretty. Very well, I'll add that your figure is
excellent and your gown shows it to advantage.'

She smiled to herself.

'And now, Kate, I do believe you have had a little
more wine than you are used to, and are feeling sleepy as
a result.'

'I am a trifle sleepy, yes.'

'Then I suggest you have a nap.'

'Mmmm . . .'

'Not like that. You cannot rest fully clothed—and that
little waist tells me you are wearing stays, which cannot
possibly be comfortable for sleeping.'

'Stays!' This woke her up. 'I am not wearing stays!'

'I do not believe you. Every woman wears stays—and
your waist is so small and smooth . . .'

'I cannot bear them. I—am—not—wearing—stays!'

'Very well. Undress for bed, and I shall see for
myself.'

'Why should you, you impertinent man? Besides, I
cannot undress without a maid.'

'Oh yes, you can. I shall help you. Turn over.'

She lay, unmoving, lazily smiling. With a laugh, he put

his hands beneath her and turned her over as if she had been a feather bolster.

'Now, young lady, we shall see!'

It was like a child's game as they struggled; Katharine too sleepy to do much more than put her hands behind her and try to fend him off, while Harry set to work on the hooks of her gown. When they were undone, he lifted her like a doll, twitched down her sleeves and thrust the gown away from her. Then he laid her back on the bed, his arm still about her, and ran the other hand gently up and down and round her waist. It was at the same time both soothing and exciting, she found. She was enjoying it, and did not move his hand away.

'I think you are wearing stays.'

'I am not.'

'Are you not? Well . . . I cannot be sure.'

'You are pretending. You know I'm not . . .'

She kicked off her shoes and drew her legs up on to the bed. That was more comfortable. Harry was undoing the ribbons of her petticoats. Without quite knowing how it happened, she found she was lying in her shift, with him stretched beside her, his hand once more exploring her waist.

His head was close to hers as he whispered, 'I do believe you are right! No stays.'

Strange and delightful sensations were running through her, as if the touch of his hands softened her muscles, turned her bones to green sticks and made her tremble and quiver within. The hands went further, and now were gently caressing her in a way she had never dreamed of, easing her shift aside so that his warm fingers could stroke and play about her naked breasts. She thought she ought to check him, but it was too much trouble when his touch was so amazingly exciting. The

points of her breasts tightened with their own individual
response, while within her a new longing awoke, a
yearning that was crying for expression; and how to
satisfy it, she did not know.

His mouth came down on hers, and that helped,
because responding to his kisses seemed to ease the
longing. Then, as Harry went on kissing her, the feeling
grew worse again, her heart was beating as if it would
burst and her breath was sobbing in her throat with the
ache of it. His body was moving, and she neither knew
nor cared why, as long as his lips and hands still worked
their magic. Suddenly a pain shot through her body,
sharp and stabbing, yet even that did not matter, for
somehow it was part of an ecstasy that was flooding her
being, a wild expression of all the excitement she felt.
She clung to him, aware that he too was in some kind of
delirium, knowing instinctively that the two of them
would somehow satisfy this glorious urgency of the
blood.

Then, all at once, it was over. There was a rushing and
then a peace within her. Harry's body left hers, and he
collapsed beside her, while she lay panting, spent, and
utterly fulfilled. Only then did she realise that what had
happened was what she had dreaded, that he had turned
the horrible and shocking business into a thing of magic
and wonder. So that was marriage. She had never
guessed . . .

Harry's voice was murmuring lazily in her ear. 'For an
innocent virgin, Kate, you did very well.'

For a second she could not believe it. What to her had
been a wonderful, incredible experience was to him just
a matter for appraisal.

Her throat tightened and swelled up. She could not
answer. She did not wish to answer. There was nothing

to be said to a man who could be a partner in such glorious moments and then speak as if it were an action for which one was given a kind of score for performance. She turned her head away from him, and let the tears run silently on to her pillow. So that was all it meant to him. Then, in future, she must see that it meant no more to her.

CHAPTER
THREE

THE DAY after the consummation of their marriage, Harry went riding alone as usual. It's as if he has done what was necessary and now cannot stand the sight of me, Katharine thought. He had been very clever. He had waited until she was tipsy and taken the opportunity of playing upon her when she was relaxed, unthinking, unaware. Perhaps he had deliberately made her tipsy with that intention. Well, it was done now. She knew what the physical process was which would lead to her fulfilling the terms of her marriage.

Life at Embercombe went on as before, but there was the exciting prospect of a visit to Bath.

'Let us have a reasonable stay before my leave is up, Mama,' Breedon said. 'I am sure that Kate is ready for society.'

'I am doing my best to prepare her.'

As a break from her gruelling sessions on etiquette and deportment, Katharine hoped for a few rides with Harry, and was more than a little put out one afternoon when he told her she could not join him.

'I am going to see the tenant at Long Farm on a matter of business,' he said. 'You would have nothing to do while we were having our discussion.'

'Couldn't I talk to the farmer's wife?'

'It would be embarrassing to her for you to arrive

without warning. They do not expect to mix with us, you know. You would be quite *de trop*.'

'So I mustn't mix with the women, and am not allowed to listen to business with the men! Am I to be granted no sociable feelings or any intelligence? Am I to be merely a doll?'

'Don't be unreasonable, Kate! Women are not fitted for business, and you cannot break down social barriers just as you see fit. You will pay visits in good time.'

'When the local gentry decide to call on me! I'm not interested in them. Don't you understand—I want to meet the real Embercombe people, to know if they need help . . .'

'Really, Kate! You must not interfere! The bailiff reports if a roof leaks or if a man is unfit for work—it is not your business.'

'Then what *is* my business?'

'To prepare yourself for our society.'

'And to produce an heir! Don't remind me of that!'

'I did not intend to. Now, if you will excuse me—I shall be only a couple of hours.'

She bade him goodbye, feeling in a very ill temper.

Since Lady Cecily was resting, Katharine was at least free from supervision and criticism; so, thwarted of her ride, she looked about for employment. At Walcotte she would probably have gone to the kitchen and made a batch of bread, taking out her annoyance in some vigorous kneading of the dough, but here nothing like that was possible. Neither could she go and pull out weeds or dig a patch of ground—that would cause utter consternation among the gardeners. She could not invade the stables and pet the horses. It was too fine a day to sit indoors reading.

Instead, she took some embroidery out into the

garden and spent some time at it. She missed Harry
more than she cared to admit—she had no point of contact with his parents. The fact that she and he frequently
ended up by arguing was a pity, but then it was usually
his fault; he would so often take the attitude that she was
trying to be equal to a man in intelligence and capability.
It wasn't so, but it annoyed her that he should think it
was not possible. Why did men think they were the lords
of creation and that women were in every way inferior?
She was quite sure it need not be thus, and would dearly
love to prove it.

Harry was late, and she was very bored. She had been
excluded from the visit, but surely there would be no
harm if she went to meet him? She knew the way he
would come. Her annoyance had by now evaporated,
and she could only think of the pleasure of a leisurely
ride back with him.

So she ordered her mare, called her maid, went
upstairs and changed into her habit. But the time she
went downstairs again the mare was outside the main
door in the care of a groom, who, it was plain, expected
to accompany her.

But she preferred to ride alone, it left her free to think
her own thoughts; she hated being dogged by servants.

'I shall not need you, Jenkins,' she said. 'I am not
going far—hardly beyond the park, I think.'

'Very well, m'lady,' he replied, not quite managing to
hide his look of surprise at her unconventionality.

The day was fine and sunny—the weather had been
exceptionally good—and beyond the parkland in the
distance she could see swaths of gold and buff which
were the ripe cornfields. Harvesting would start any day
now, she thought. She rode through the park. The deer
of the Embercombe herd lifted their heads at the move-

ment of her passage, but she was far enough away not to startle them, and they soon resumed cropping the lush grass.

Although she reached the park boundary, there was still no sign of Harry. The ride was very enjoyable, and she had no intention of turning back yet. She went through the lodge gates, opened for her with a curtsy by the keeper's wife, out on to the road, turning in the direction of Wells. Harry could not be far away now. This was not the main road yet; it ran beside the park for some distance before reaching the turnpike. It was narrow and hedge-bordered, casting through fields dotted here and there with spinneys of hazel.

A few minutes later she heard the sound of a trotting horse. Her heart gave a little bounce of joy—it must be Harry, taking the last stage of his journey very easily, by the sound of it. She rounded a bend and saw the rider approaching only a short distance away. To her disgust it was not Harry—but Richard Stukely.

As he came abreast, he put out a hand and caught her reins.

'Well, Katharine, have you nothing to say to me?'

Her mare shied at being so abruptly pulled up, and she quietened her, at the same time flashing Stukely a glance and saying, 'Nothing! Let go of my reins.'

To her surprise and relief he did so. He was smiling at her—if you could call it a smile, for it was calculating, gloating, and most unpleasant.

'We'll ride together,' he said. 'Whichever way you choose to go—it's all the same to me.'

She could not prevent him from riding beside her, no matter which direction she took. It would be best to turn back, rather than distance herself further from Ember-combe—and with luck she could take him unawares, set

spurs to her mare and outdistance him. She turned and
began to ride away.

'That's uncommon civil of you, my dear.'

He kept pace with her. She supposed he was doing it
to irritate her, but she had no intention of putting up
with his boorish behaviour. She would get rid of him. He
would hardly have the insolence to ride cross-country
over Embercome land—but there was no reason why
she should not take a short cut across the fields to avoid
him. She saw a gap in the hedge; there were rails across
it, but the ground was level on either side, and she urged
her mare to it. They jumped it cleanly, to continue
across the corner of the field.

Katharine heard him take the jump just behind her.
Curse the man and his insolence! So he intended to
follow her as far as the park. Very well, she would give
him a run for his money. She was still only aware of his
effrontery; she had no perception as yet of any danger.

His big hunter came pounding up behind her.

'You'll not get away from me!' he laughed. 'Did you
think that little mare could outpace my Rory?'

Without replying, she struck out into the field to pass
the other side of an encroaching coppice. Now he was
abreast of her, and glancing up she saw his face, the full
lips grinning, the eyes holding such a look of evil delight
that a stab of fear shot through her. Again he grabbed
her reins, this time in earnest. She struck at his hand, but
he pulled her horse up, and still holding her reins he
shook his feet out of his stirrups and flung himself out of
his saddle. The next moment his hand was on her arm.

She hit at his arm with her riding-whip, but it was
useless. He had no intention of letting her go—and a
moment later he had dragged her from her horse. She
stumbled, regained her feet and continued to strike at

him. Her raised whip caught her mare's flank, she took fright, threw up her head and cantered off. Stukely's hunter stood by quietly enough as the two of them struggled.

'That's what I like! A bit of spirit! But it'll do you no good, my girl! I'll have my revenge for the way you've treated me!'

He caught her whip, and twisted it in her grasp so that she had to let go. Casting it aside, he took her by the shoulders and threw her to the ground. He's going to beat me the way my father did, she thought, and her flesh cringed. She had not yet raised her voice, but now things had gone far enough. There was little hope of anyone being in earshot, but as she tried to scramble to her feet, she let out a cry for help.

The next thing she knew, he had flung himself on the ground beside her, forcing her back and clamping a hand over her mouth. His eyes, slaty-blue and bloodshot, glared down at her from a foot away.

'We can do without an audience for what I have in mind!'

His heavy body was lying half over hers, and only then did she realise his intention, as with his free hand he began to fumble with the flap of his breeches. Now she struggled wildly, twisting her body to and fro and trying to claw him with her nails, but he seized her wrists, forced her arms behind her, pulled up her riding-skirt and wound her arms in it, then held her own weight on them.

'I'd cover your head to keep you quiet!' he gloated, 'But I want to see your face, to watch how you like it when I'm taking my fill of pleasure from you . . .'

She caught her breath and screamed as loudly as she could—and his vile mouth came down on hers and stopped her cries. His breath, tainted, stinking, was hot in her nostrils, his ill-shaven cheek was rasping hers, his hand was pawing at her body. Now she was mad with fear and horror, her flesh crawling with revulsion, her heart pumping with terror, and she still tried to shake him off. But it was hopeless. He was so strong and heavy, and was crushing her breath and all chance of resistance out of her. With the skirt of her habit pulled up he was now tugging at her underclothes, and his knees had forced themselves between her legs.

He raised his head to pant exultantly at her, 'Now I've got you, you little bitch! Now you'll pay for your arrogance! I'll have as much as I want from you . . .'

Nothing could stop him now. He laughed in her face.

'So I wasn't good enough for you! You'll find I'm as good as any man at this! And when you have a brat, maybe you won't know if it's your precious husband's or Richard Stukely's!'

She gave one wild despairing shriek. There could be nothing worse than this—to be violated, possessed by force and by a man so utterly loathsome! Her senses were leaving her, although she was still resisting, there was nothing, nothing she could do to save herself. She was sobbing and crying out, and his face was grinning down at hers in triumph, the bloodshot eyes gloating, the flabby lips oozing slobber, the reddened cheeks, blue-jowled, flushing deeper with the strength of his lust. The hand that had bared her thighs now violated her.

'That's good! You know what comes now . . .'

She knew. The next second his body would complete the conquest, and what would follow would plunge her into the foulest depths of degradation.

And then—then, amazingly, there were confused

sounds near by, and Stukely paused, checked himself, and looked swiftly about him. Then his body jerked itself away from hers. Sobbing and gasping in incredulous relief, she rolled over in the grass under the hazel spinney, fighting her way out of the constricting folds of her skirt, pulling it down and curling herself into a ball, her face buried in the turf, sick with shame and disgust. She heard the sound of blows. Turning her head, she saw from the corner of her eye that Stukely was scrambling to his horse; he mounted anyhow and rode off hell for leather, while Harry Breedon threw himself on the ground beside her.

He held her in his arms, cradled against his chest, and spoke in a voice so hoarse that she hardly recognised it.

'Kate! Kate! How badly are you hurt? How far did . . .'

He could not finish.

'More frightened—than hurt—he did not quite—succeed . . .'

'I'll kill him! You poor child—I would have killed him then, but I had to see you.'

'Thank God you came—oh, thank God you came!'

He held her until her sobs subsided and she was more in control of herself.

'Who was it, Kate? Do you know?'

'It was Stukely, of course.'

'*Stukely!* My God . . . Can you ride, Kate? I caught your mare—I thought you had been thrown—then I heard you scream. Can you . . . ?'

'I'll manage.'

Harry helped her to mount, and they rode in silence back to Embercombe. She felt she could not bear to talk of it. His face was set and grim, his mouth a hard line, his eyes glinting from under contracted brows. She had never seen him look like that before. He too seemed beyond words, containing all his revulsion and fury within him.

When they reached home, he supported her as they went indoors.

'Take me to my room, Harry.'

'Not yet, Kate. My father must hear of this from you, at once.'

Harry overruled her protests and led her to where the Embercombes were taking their ease and sipping cups of chocolate. His father looked up sharply. 'What? Has the girl had a spill?' he asked taking in Katharine's dishevelled state.

'No,' said Harry grimly. 'Stukely tried to rape her.'

There was a gasp from Lady Cecily. 'Tried? He did not . . .? Then heaven be praised!'

Harry had seen Katharine to a chair, and now stood beside her, one arm about her shoulders. The Earl seemed dumbfounded.

'Tried—to *rape* her? In God's name, the fellow must be a lunatic! Here, m'dear, give the girl a cup of chocolate.'

'No,' said Harry shortly. 'I'll give her some brandy.'

Katharine began to feel a little hysterical. *Chocolate!* A cup of chocolate was to put everything right! Harry came back from the tantalus as Lady Cecily turned to Katharine.

'You are quite sure he did not . . . It would be so dreadful if . . .'

Katharine gave a little sobbing laugh. She's thinking how embarrassing it would be if I had Stukely's child —polluting the Embercombe bloodline—and then she found she could not stop sobbing. Harry held her tightly and put a glass to her lips.

'Hush, Kate! Try not to break down. You've been very brave. Now tell my father what happened.'

She drank some brandy, then pressed the back of her hand against her lips and fought for self-control.

'I met him—in the lane. He insisted on riding with me. I tried to get away by cutting across the field, but he followed me. Then—then he pulled me off my horse . . .'

'It is almost incredible!' Lady Cecily exclaimed.

'He got away—I had to see to Kate,' Harry went on. 'I'd like to settle with him myself, but I suppose we had better go to the Justice.'

His parents exchanged a quick look.

'I hardly think . . .' the Earl began.

'You would not really want that,' Lady Cecily said swiftly. 'Think what it would entail. Katharine would have to give evidence—the whole county would know —and eventually *everyone*—and he did not actually succeed . . . and of course he would fight it.'

'You know what that would mean, my boy,' continued the Earl. 'Stukely would have no scruples. He would say that Katharine led him on, and then objected when things went a little too far.'

'Yes,' Lady Cecily agreed. 'And it would seem very strange, that it happened off the road—in the field, you say.'

Katharine listened in incredulous silence. They were going to do nothing. They were too concerned with the possible scandal. All they wanted was to hush the matter up.

'But, Father, no one could suspect Katharine . . .'

'There's no evidence, my boy. It would be her word against his. You must see what the result would be.'

Oh, yes, she could see, if Breedon couldn't. A bench

—of men—a jury, perhaps, of men—all saying to themselves, Well, she was probably a tease . . . they went into
the field . . . then she thought better of it, and he didn't
even manage to finish the job—no reason to punish him,
he only wanted a bit of fun . . .

'I see what you mean. It would be very unpleasant for
Kate.'

Katharine found her voice. 'Unpleasant What I have
just endured was more than *unpleasant*! Surely I am the
one who should decide whether I can stand a trial? And
is he to go scot-free?'

'You cannot consider it!' Lady Cecily said sharply.
'You cannot shame yourself further and disgrace us.'

'Shame *myself! I disgrace you!* What have *I* done . . .'

'Mama did not mean that,' Breedon said quickly. 'She
simply wishes to avoid the gossip and scandalmongering
it would cause—and the ordeal you would suffer. I
understand why we cannot take Stukely to law.'

She looked from one to the other, and saw the matter
was settled. She struggled to her feet, and spoke as
slowly and unemotionally as she was able.

'I see. I can understand how you men view the matter.
After all, men do these things, and you cannot run the
risk of having to *suffer* them, so it means nothing to you.
But you, Lady Cecily—I would have hoped for something better. If women will not support women, what
hope is there? I am sorry that by my mere existence I
have brought scandal to your doorstep. It was foolish of
me to look for any understanding, any sympathy, any
support.'

She found she was still clutching a half-empty glass.
Her self-control broke. 'You offer me a cup of chocolate! You give me a glass of brandy! A recompense for
being raped! *Keep it!*'

With one furious gesture she flung the glass from her into the fireplace. A horrified silence followed the shivering tinkle of shattering glass, and she turned away.

Breedon started towards her.

'*No!* Leave me alone!'

She picked up the trailing skirt of her habit and walked out of the room without giving any of them another glance.

They were on their way to Bath. The society, the diversions Katharine had been promised were about to materialise, and she was very thankful. Life at Embercombe had become almost insupportable to her, for the day-to-day monotony had given her every opportunity to brood on her recent experience.

On the night of Stukely's attack she had been like an automaton, sitting motionless, all animation suspended, speaking only when spoken to and that in monosyllables. She could summon no strength, no energy, and her mind was constantly reliving the hideous moments when she had been totally in Stukely's power. She prepared for bed in silence, Harry watching her anxiously. When he was in bed beside her, he did not blow out the candles but looked down at her and spoke with a suppressed urgency.

'Kate, you cannot go on like this. Storm at me—weep —do something—anything—but do not contain it all within yourself.'

'Let me sleep—if I can. There's nothing to say.'

She would not look at him. He took her chin in his hands and turned her face to his.

'You must let yourself go, Kate. Listen to me. I know that in cases such as this women have a lot to complain of. But though my parents may have the wrong reasons, they are right in saying we must not go to law. It would be an appalling experience for you, and it would do no good, only harm.'

She shut her eyes and presented him with the features of a mask. He put his arm about her and drew her stiff body to lie on his chest, one hand stroking her hair, his lips pressed to her forehead.

'Don't hate me, Kate. I will be a husband to you in more than one sense. I'll not let you go unrevenged.'

She did not answer.

'There was nothing I could do, *then*,' he went on insistently. 'I had to see to you, though what I wanted to do was to get my pistol from my saddle-holster and blow his brains out. Now you must leave me to settle with Stukely in my own way.'

He moved and lifted her face to his. 'Open your eyes. Look at me.'

Slowly, reluctantly she did so.

'Do you believe me?'

'I believe you are sorry for me. But whatever you do, I cannot believe anything can punish Stukely, or wipe out my degradation.'

'Don't think of it like that. You were not degraded —only Stukely, who behaved worse than an animal. You are yourself, and you will not be crushed by any man's action, any sordid circumstance.

The great knot of tension within her began to loosen a little. 'Do you really think that?'

'Yes. I wouldn't lie to you. You've had a shock, but you're brave and strong. You'll get over it, given time, and be right as rain.'

A lump rose in her throat. One man was kind to her. He was trying to help. Her body went limp in his arms and at last the tears came. But she did not think there was anything he could do.

Three days later he came in from riding, looking dishevelled and triumphant. Katharine met him on the terrace, and he flung an arm round her.

'Well, I've done it, Kate. I've taught Stukely his lesson.'

She turned to him in swift surprise. 'What did you do?'

'I've been waiting to catch him riding alone. This morning, there he was—and I gave him the biggest horsewhipping you could imagine. I'm glad to say he couldn't mount his horse when I'd finished—had to cling to the stirrup and let it drag him home. He'll be abed for days.'

'Won't he have you charged?'

'Not he! Admit that he's been horsewhipped? He'll keep it very quiet.'

'Oh, Harry—thank you! But now he will be your enemy as well as mine.'

'And much good will that do him. I told him that one word from him about you and I'd repeat the dose. What's more, I warned him that if he ever attempted to lay so much as a finger on you again I would personally shoot him—not in a duel, but pistol him down like the mad dog he is. I don't think we shall have any more trouble from Richard Stukely.'

Katharine suspected that it was due to Harry's urging that they were going to Bath, although Lady Cecily took the credit for prescribing the visit as a cure for her low spirits. Whoever was the instigator was not important; the fact was that they were on their way. Harry travelled on horseback, and Katherine was closed with his parents in the Embercombe coach. She did not like it as well as Harry's travelling coach; it was larger, heavier,

clumsier, and not so well sprung. It looked a splendid
conveyance with its gleaming paintwork decorated with
coats-of-arms and coronets, the hammercloth over the
coachman's seat lavishly trimmed with gold braid and
tassels; but it lumbered along the rutted roads at a
walking pace most of the time, and only when they
struck a good stretch of turnpike road could the four
horses manage to break into a trot. So it took them a
long time to reach 'The Bath'.

The countryside was lovely, the villages through
which they passed looked reasonably clean and prosper-
ous, the weather was fine, and they had no serious
mishaps. Once a wheel got caught in a rut and the coach
was stuck, perched at a precarious angle; they all had to
get out, and it took half an hour of sweating and straining
and cursing by coachman and footmen to persuade the
horses to get the coach moving again, but that, and later
on a broken trace, was all they suffered, so they were
very lucky. They spent one night at a good inn, and left
quite early. Chilcompton, Radstock, Peasedown St
John were all behind them now, and they were on
the last stage of their journey, passing through rolling
country in the late afternoon sun. Then they were
rattling along the top of a hill, from which viewpoint
Katharine, craning out of a window, decided she could
at last see Bath.

It lay in the cup of surrounding hills, held within the
curve of the River Avon, a jumble of buildings around
the grey bulk of the abbey church. Here and there were
patches of creamy-yellow amid the grey; they must be all
the fine new buildings Lord Embercombe had told her
about. During the present century Bath had become
very fashionable, and there had been much rebuilding to
accommodate the visitors who flocked there for pleasure

and amusement as well as the cure. Richard 'Beau' Nash, the 'King of Bath', had now been dead some years, but his rules were still enforced. The architects were planning more and yet more splendid, buildings to enhance the city.

Lord Embercombe told Katharine that he had previously rented a house for his visits, but a couple of years ago they had liked the season so well that he had thought it worth while to buy a house.

'Deuced inconvenient, those old places. Drains stink, and not room to swing a cat. But that new architect fellow Wood has been putting up some very tolerable houses. I decided it was worth me while to have one when I saw the elegant square he was setting up. Queen Square, it's called. A nice little house, suits us for a short season.'

They had reached some outlying houses and the way led down a hill of alarming steepness. She heard the coachman apply the brakes and shout to the horses. Driving down the hill in a large heavy coach with four horses to be managed was a frightening experience. But Briggs had skill, and at last they reached the bottom, the brakes were taken off, and the sweating horses clattered across the bridge.

Katharine felt a touch of disappointment. Bath looked just like any other town. Southgate Street was narrow—its dirty cobbles edged with small old buildings, some rather ramshackle, some doing their best to be presentable shops of a very ordinary type. The side streets were even narrower, and gave glimpses of mean dwellings that looked quite wretched. It was no better than the older, poorer parts of Wells. The street was littered with rubbish, and full of people on foot and on horseback, with market carts and drays and barrows

choking the way. Progress was slow; she had plenty of
time to see that the houses, at first only standing on the
right side, now hemmed them in on both, and then
began to get slightly larger, less neglected—and there
was the abbey, dominating everything, over on their
right.

Now they reached a crossing, which was even more
choked with traffic. Later she discovered it was West-
gate Street, and carried everything moving between
London and Bristol. It took much time, and a lot of
sweating, shouting and swearing on the part of Briggs to
get the coach across, and when they had done so, with no
more trouble than an upended barrow-load of chickens
and an obviously deaf old man frightened out of his
wits, they had a narrow lane with an upward slope to
negotiate.

At the end, the way was wider. Here the street
opposite was in process of being built, some fine houses
on either side were already finished, others were coming
on, and Katharine could appreciate that the new buildings of Bath were going to give the town a very different
appearance. They were all of stone, with no visible
beams at all, the window frames and doors being the
only external timber; they were simple—'classical' was
the term, Harry had said—with an impressive austerity.
This was Milsom Street—it was some time before
Katharine learnt all the names—and its width was at
present somewhat illusory as traffic had to negotiate
piles of stone and other building materials that at present
encroached upon it. But this the Embercombe coach did
not have to do; they turned left along Wood Street,
where fairly small houses soon gave way to larger ones,
and then, all at once, the vista opened, and they were in
Queen Square.

To Katharine's country-bred mind it consisted simply of four terraces of houses formed into a square with a cobbled centre, but the whole effect was incomparably spacious and dignified. The Embercombe house lay on the best side—the north—and as they drove up to it the mellow stone was bathed in late afternoon sunshine. The ground floor was plain, but the doors were rather fine; and above the ground floor tall Corinthian pillars soared the height of two more storeys, with rows of windows set between them, and above the cornice the central houses had a severely plain pediment which gave the whole terrace the effect of being a unity, like the front of a palace. One hardly noticed from ground level that there was yet another storey, for the sloping roof held little dormer windows; these would light the servants' bedrooms.

As Katharine climbed down gratefully from the coach, stiff with sitting and sore from being jolted about, Harry came to the door to welcome them.

'So, Mama! You have made good time.'

'*We came down the Hollow Way!* What did you mean by it, Briggs? I shall have something to say to you later! We are safe and sound, thank heaven, Harry, and greatly in need of refreshment.' She swept her wide skirts through the doorway.

Harry turned to his wife, and took her arm. 'Well, Kate!' he said with a smile of greeting. 'Welcome to Bath!'

CHAPTER
FOUR

ON THE next morning, Katharine's initiation to society began with a visit to the town. They went to the Pump Room, and Lacy Cecily insisted they should go every morning to take the waters. 'It is important for you, Katharine,' she said, when her son's wife was less than enthusiastic about draining a glassful of water with a strange metallic flavour.

'But I am perfectly well,' she protested.

'So I hope. The waters are of particular value for young wives.'

Lady Cecily's meaning look was enough. So the waters, in addition to benefiting gout, rheumatism and the consumption—and countless other ills—were also reputed to encourage fertility. Katharine found this hard to believe, but at least they could do no harm.

Visiting the Pump Room was an experience in itself. Katharine had never seen so many people with varying signs of illness congregating before, in the company of quite as many other people who were in good health and even better spirits and intent on enjoying themselves to the full. ·The poor invalids, having been wheeled in chairs to some convenient place and given a glass of spa water, were largely ignored, and left to exchange with each other long tales of illnesses suffered and cures hoped for. The healthy element busied themselves with gossip and flirtation, taking snuff with ceremony, eating comfits from little silver boxes, casting seductive glances over fans or ogling through quizzing-glasses, while they tried to decide what should be done next to relieve boredom.

There was, of course, The Bath. Lady Cecily recommended it to Katharine, but agreed she could be a spectator before taking part in the bathing. Katharine followed where she was led, and emerged on to a kind of stone gallery overlooking a large bathing-pool. She had no idea what to expect, and what she saw both amazed and shocked her.

The steaming green waters were full of people of both sexes, the ladies wearing calico bath gowns, the men apparently naked. For the majority, the bath was plainly not a matter of solemn immersion in the waters for the sake of one's health, but rather a licence for amusement and horseplay. The women, of all ages, shapes and sizes, were bobbing about, quite reckless of the fact that their wet gowns were most revealing, the clinging cloth putting their breasts on full display and in some cases, when the gown was loose, swinging aside in the water and not covering the bosom at all. Katharine could swear that some of the women were deliberately revealing their ample charms. They laughed and chattered, pushing before them floating japanned bowls which contained sweetmeats and toilet necessaries. Their squeals and shrieks of protest at the men's attentions, which varied from teasing and staring to actually handling the women's bodies in a manner ostensibly playful but positively lewd, all rang quite false and served to encourage more than to deter. She could hardly believe her eyes.

When she turned her attention to the spectators in the

gallery, she saw that only a few were behaving in a
dignified manner like the Embercombes. The few
women seemed to be old and raddled, and doing their
best to engage the men's attentions; but the men were
either old lechers or young ones, bucks and dandies,
making the most of the opportunity to scrutinise the
women in the bath. There was a constant interplay
between the spectators and the bathers of shouted exchanges, coarse remarks and lewd jokes; it was inde-
scribably noisy, bawdy, sensual and gross, and gave
Katharine no pleasure or amusement. To her surprise
Lady Cecily, though looking somewhat disapproving,
expressed no shock; everyone but herself seemed to take
the goings-on for granted.

Katharine looked about her at the fashionable company. How stiff and unnatural the people seemed. The
women's faces were powdered white, their floury cheeks
circled with rouge, so that they looked for all the world
like animated puppets. The men were little better; their
gestures and voices equally affected, they too were
dressed-up marionettes in their damask coats and
embroidered waistcoats. She had thought Harry rather
finely dressed in his town clothes, but against this company he looked unpretentious and manly.

Lady Cecily had already met a group of people
with whom she was acquainted; now she introduced
Katharine. The girl made her curtsies to her elders and
behaved exactly as she had been taught, then let the
small-talk play around her as she contrived to look at the
general scene. Her glance fell on a man standing at the
parapet near by. He was taller than average, and richly
dressed even for this company. As she looked, she heard
him remark to his companion, a shorter, foppish-
looking fellow,

'Egad, there's nothing worth watching this morning. Let's away.'

He turned, and saw Katharine. Raising his quizzing-glass, he gazed at her. She looked away, but was aware of his continued stare. Then, although he lowered his voice a little, his next remark was quite audible to her.

'Faith, I was wrong! There's a delicious little morsel, as simple as a milkmaid! I must find out who she is.'

He sauntered across, threading his way until he reached them. He gave an elaborate bow and addressed the Countess. 'Egad, Lady Cecily! You have risen like the sun on our horizon! What a pleasure to see you!'

'Why, Lord Carbern! How do you do?'

Now the man turned to Harry. 'Well, Stonebridge, so you are not at sea, defending our realm! Squiring the ladies instead, eh?'

'Good morning, Carbern,' Harry replied, with polite indifference.

Lady Cecily now introduced Katharine.

'My son has married at last, Lord Carbern. This is Katharine, his wife.'

'Lud, Lady Katharine! I am overwhelmed! Bath will be all the brighter for such beauty! Will you be staying long?'

'As long as Lady Cecily requires, Lord Carbern,' she said coolly.

'Then we must see that the stay is a long one, Lady Cecily! Bath requires the society of two such charming ladies, and, Stonebridge, you must be sociable, positively you must. Though newly-wed, you must not keep your bride to yourself!'

What lay beneath that affected manner? Katharine wondered. The eyes were hard, the mouth thin-lipped;

she suspected selfishness, cruelty even. But apart from a
nose rather too large and hooked, he was good-looking,
he had a presence, and unbounded self-confidence.

Now another voice broke in on her thoughts. It was
high and light, the tones altogether too sweet, too
studiedly feminine.

'Why, Hawwy!' it said. 'What a tewwific supwise! We
thought you had weally quite forgotten us!'

She turned to look at the owner of the voice. It was a
young lady with golden hair elaborately dressed, a
plump face with dimpled cheeks and blue eyes, and a
generously rounded figure, all curves and softness.
Quite artificial, Katharine thought—and to her amazement heard Harry answer with every appearance of
pleasure.

'Annabel! This is delightful! You are looking very
well. And how is Harcourt?'

'Oh, poow dawling, he is afflicted with his wetched
gout. He is taking the waters for it with the utmost
wegulawity.'

'Then let us hope they will be of benefit. Annabel,
may I introduce my wife, Katharine?'

'Your *wife*! Why, Hawwy, so it is weally twue you awe
mawwied! We heard a wumour—how vewwy unexpected!'

By looking at Katharine during the last phrase she
managed to imply that she was a surprising choice—but
they greeted each other with formal politeness. Harry
still looked as if he took pleasure in the encounter.
Heaven help me, Kate thought, if that is the sort of
woman he prefers—a simpering ninny who cannot or
will not pronounce a single 'r'.

Lord Carbern had not left them, and he now
addressed Katharine again.

'Lady Kate, you positively must bathe! Join us tomorrow morning—let us all take a dip in the bath—you will look a veritable naiad, a Venus rising from the water to delight the eyes of mere mortal men! I can hardly wait for such a delicious sight!'

His words and his attitude infuriated her. Harry, who looked as if he considered Carbern's words as so much nonsense not worth a reply, said nothing. She answered coldly,

'If I bathe, Lord Carbern, it will be for my own benefit and not for your amusement.'

He laughed as if she had said something witty.

'Stonebridge, your wife has a sharp tongue! In my admiration did I say anything to deserve a rebuke?'

'I have no idea.'

'Lady Kate, why are you so harsh with me? You are not offended?'

'Not at all, my lord. And I was not harsh. If ever you offend me I shall speak much more strongly.'

'How delightful! A young lady of spirit! Lady Cecily, what do you do this evening? Shall we see you at the Assembly Rooms?'

Later, Lady Cecily issued Katharine a word of warning.

'I must tell you, child, that manners at The Bath are somewhat lax. You must be circumspect. As a young bride, you must not risk a bad reputation. Do not become friendly with bloods like young Carbern. By the way, do you intend to bathe?'

'Indeed, no, Lady Cecily,' she replied. 'From what I saw, I care neither for the company nor the behaviour, nor do I think it good to enter water which holds so many other bodies—some of them, I venture, not being too clean when they arrive.'

'Tush! You are a fastidious girl! The water cures everything.'

Katharine had also seen more than one bather with a most unpleasant skin affection, and this was another discouragement to her. She replied, 'Let us hope so. But since I am healthy, I do not consider I need it. I will drink the water in the Pump Room, since you wish it, but I do not feel obliged to bathe.'

Lady Cecily let the subject drop, and Katharine had the feeling that although she herself was used to and condoned the behaviour at The Bath, she did not necessarily relish the idea of her son's wife taking part.

All Bath society gathered at the Assembly Rooms, so it was not surprising that on their first evening visit the Embercombes met the Harcourts. Annabel was in her element, gaining plenty of attention; she was liberally decked with jewels, and wearing a wide-panniered and very low-cut gown which showed a perilous amount of her very plump breasts. Lord Harcourt was considerably older than his wife; a red-faced stout gentleman in dark violet, heavily embroidered in greens and purples, topped with a large old-fashioned grey wig. One foot was heavily padded and bandaged, and he moved with difficulty on the arm of a manservant. Katharine noticed that Annabel, having seen him to the card-room, did not stay, but came out to join the dancers.

Harry found Katharine a partner, a young man named Spenlow who seemed a pleasant harmless fellow, and went off to dance with Annabel. When the dance ended, Spenlow led her to a chair next to a rather plain, thin-faced, dark girl whom he introduced as his sister Sophia. At first Katharine thought Miss Spenlow stand-offish, but since there was no sign of Harry she decided to make the best of her; when she continued with conversation, she realised that the girl was in fact pain-fully shy. She tried to draw her out, asking about the diversions of Bath.

'What do you find most enjoyable here, Miss Spenlow?'

The girl's face brightened; smiling, she looked much less plain. 'Oh, the music! I am devoted to Mr Handel's works. The concerts here are quite excellent. They are directed by Mr Herschel.'

'I am afraid I have not heard of him. I have spent my life in the country until now. Please tell me about him.'

'He is a very gifted and unusual man. He actually has a telescope pointing out of his window so that he can observe the stars!'

'I would have thought an enormous ear-trumpet, in order to catch the music of the spheres—which everyone believes in but no one has heard—would be more appropriate!'

Katharine half-expected her joke to fall flat, but Sophia laughed.

'Lady Kate, how delightful!'

They were soon quite at ease.

There was no shortage of partners, for Katharine, although she had only one dance with Harry: it was not 'done' to dance often with one's wife. She could not avoid dancing with Lord Carbern, but under his bold eyes and pressing manner once was enough; when she saw him coming towards her again she quickly accepted Herbert Spenlow's hand.

Spenlow, she discovered, was quite a chatterbox.

'Is it true, Lady Katharine, that you and Stonebridge eloped to Gretna Green?'

'Quite true.'

'And I presume Harry will now give up the sea?'

'I hardly think so. He is making at least one more voyage.'

'Extraordinary man! I cannot imagine,' Spenlow continued, 'how Stonebridge, with the advantages of his family, wealth, a title and a good presence, should prefer doctoring a crew of dirty, louse-ridden sailors in the extreme discomfort of the high seas and with no prospect of promotion, to passing a diverting life on dry land with the amusements of society. Now that he has so charming a wife, it is even more inexplicable.'

Katharine only just managed to conceal her surprise. Doctoring! She had heard nothing of that. She spoke as lightly as she could. 'It is never possible to understand another person's preferences, surely?'

She sipped the glass of wine he had brought her. She could not help glancing over to where Harry and Annabel were enjoying a tête-à-tête. Herbert Spenlow followed her look.

'I see Annabel is still doing her best to recapture Harry's affections,' he said slyly.

He might have added, 'and succeeding', if he had not been speaking to me, Katharine thought.

'She is welcome to try,' she retorted lightly.

'You sound as confident as you have every right to be! Annabel, I think, must be furious with herself for not having had more patience.'

'What do you mean by that?'

'Oh, I thought you must know! It is a rather piquant situation!'

He smiled maliciously.

'Harry was very partial to Annabel a few years ago, and would have married her. She was by no means averse to him, but at that time he had no prospect of title or fortune. Imagine Annabel as the wife of a mere naval surgeon! Obviously *she* could not, for she let her parents arrange her marriage with Harcourt. Being the Countess of Harcourt was much more to her taste, even if she had an old man for a husband. Then, of all things, Harry's brother was foolish enough to get himself killed, and *voilà*—Harry is Viscount Stonebridge, with a fortune and the prospect of an earldom! Annabel is a lively young woman, and I cannot imagine that Harcourt gives her any pleasure between the sheets, however much he may derive himself. She had much better have waited for Harry, and settled for being a viscountess now and a countess later.'

'I see. Well, she is too late now.'

'Then let me give you a word of warning, Lady Kate. If you are one of the few women nowadays who value a husband's fidelity, and do not wish to be free to pursue your own pleasures, watch for Annabel. She needs a healthy man; she has a fancy for Harry, and she will steal your husband with no more compunction than she'd have in sticking a patch on her face.'

It was all so casually and airily said. Society apparently made a joke of such things. Katharine gave a little laugh.

'She will find that difficult when Harry is on the high seas.'

'Stap me, yes! I had forgotten that!'

In the matter of information gained, her evening had been fruitful. Some of it Katharine decided to keep to herself, but Herbert Spenlow had aroused her curiosity enough to make her venture a remark or two to Harry as they were preparing for bed.

'You did not tell me you were a doctor.'

'I am not a doctor. I suppose Spenlow has been romancing. I am a naval surgeon, which is a very different thing.'

'How is that?'

'I have very little concern with illness. My main job is to amputate limbs which have been severely injured by accident or in battle, to treat wounds, and to see to men during and immediately after a flogging. That is not doctoring.'

'Why did you join the Navy?'

'Great heavens, why? I had always, as a small boy, thought of the sea as a splendidly adventurous life, and when I realised that my brother would inherit and there was little for me on land, I persuaded my father to let me join as a midshipman. I am sure he believed that one voyage would cure me.'

'But it did not.'

'It very nearly did! It knocked all the illusions out of me.'

'How did you become a naval surgeon?'

'More or less by accident. It was something that had to be done, and I found I could do it. I have little head for naval tactics, but when men are hurt in battle, someone must patch them up; it is a constructive role of a kind. Yet it is unsatisfactory, for with more knowledge one feels so much more could be done.'

He was divesting himself of his clothes, and talking almost absent-mindedly as he did so. She wanted him to tell her more.

'But you had some training?'

'I went to a naval hospital, for what it was worth. Surgeons are only just beginning to realise that our knowledge is limited and our methods crude; men are making discoveries, but it will be a very long time before their knowledge penetrates naval practice.'

'Is it true that you have no chance of promotion?'

'You are full of questions tonight! Has someone been

gossiping? Yes, it is true. A surgeon is not a fighting officer.'

'Then why do you stay, now that . . .'

'Now that I am heir to Embercombe? It is my way of life.'

He climbed into bed beside her.

'Does not your father need you to help him run the estates?'

'Egad, no! *He* does not run them—he has bailiffs for that.'

'That is a pity. I am sure, if the estates were mine, I should want to supervise what went on.'

Harry laughed. 'You had better ask him to appoint you as an extra bailiff.'

'Why do you always laugh when I take an interest in any serious subject? It is most provoking of you.'

'I do not mean to provoke. It is curious to find a girl who is interested in matters outside the house, that is all.'

'I don't see that it is any more curious than a man who is heir to great estates leaving them to serve in the Navy.'

'The Navy is a different kettle of fish from any mere household—or any estate. You really must accept that women's concerns are not the same as men's—both in their nature and their importance.'

Katharine felt anger rising within her, and wondered why it should irritate her so much to find that he held the same views as all other men. She turned to look at him and found he was leaning on one elbow and gazing down at her.

'Young Spenlow was paying great court to you today,' he said. 'But since you are above feminine matters, I opine you will not make the mistake of taking him seriously.'

I am surprised you noticed, she thought, you were so busy with Annabel! But all she said was, 'There is no likelihood of that. His compliments come much too easily, and as thick as daisies in a meadow.'

'Well, I dare say you deserve a few of them,' he conceded. 'You are looking quite handsome.'

He picked up a lock of her hair, and coiled the silky red-brown tress over his fingers.

'Nor do you have to resort to the dye-pot for this. That will make plenty of other women jealous.'

'Do you think so?'

'I am sure of it. I know something about women.'

Not enough to stop you being a fool over me, she thought, remembering again how he had been paying court to Annabel. 'I do admit that I know nothing about men,' she continued.

He began to stroke her hair and her shoulders.

'Since I shall have to leave you soon, I shall trust to your good sense not to be fooled by fellows like young Spenlow—or worse.'

He bent his head and kissed her, and against her will she felt her pulses quicken. She told herself he was not really making love to her, he was going through a practised routine in order to provide himself with an heir. Now his mouth left hers and slid down to press kisses under her chin, down her throat; his hands began to caress her. Her body started to respond, but her mind kept telling her that every action of his must be calculated, and to let him think she enjoyed it was somehow degrading. Yet her heart was beating faster, her breath coming more quickly. She tensed, and pulled away from him a little.

'Why, Kate, I thought you enjoyed love-making.'

'I cannot forget that your whole concern is to get

an heir—so you even took advantage of my being
tipsy . . .'

'Took advantage! Kate, do me a little justice! I could
have taken you by force at any time after our marriage,
but you were a virgin, with no notion of love-making,
and I waited for a good moment for the first time. You
were a little in your cups, I agree, but that made you
relaxed and heedless. It should have made it better for
you.'

He drew her close again, and excitement rose in spite
of her apprehension. He bent over to kiss her throat, his
hand began once more to stroke her arm, her shoulder,
her back, and the delicious sensation seemed to send the
tightness ebbing away from her body.

'By God, Kate! Heir or no heir, we're well matched,
and you'll be my woman—now and always—but now
—*now* . . .'

Her arm slid round him, over warm skin and hard
muscle. She was dazed, delirious, glorying in the
strength of him and in her own ability to respond. And
afterwards she lay in the darkness, thinking. It had
nothing to do with wine. Why was such an odd proceed-
ing so ecstatic, so wonderful? Yet with anyone else it
would not be so. With someone like Stukely it would be
horrible. Then why with Harry? She visualised his face,
thinking, How I would love to stroke that slightly hol-
lowed cheek, to kiss that firm mouth as he lies asleep.
Why, what a fool she was. She had fallen in love with
him!

The next morning as she prepared to go out to the Pump
Room, Harry came in and without preamble said
abruptly, 'I trust you do not intend to bathe this
morning?'

Katharine felt considerably nettled, for she had heard Annabel considering the possibility of bathing, and he had said not a word against it. So although she had no intention of so doing, she replied, 'And why should I not? Your mother suggested it.'

For a moment he did not answer. Then, 'I do not care that you should.'

'I find that rather strange. You raised no objection to Lady Annabel.'

'Annabel is not my wife. I have no right or control over her actions.'

'If you had, I doubt whether you would exert it. I opine you enjoy seeing her ample charms as much as she likes displaying them.'

'That remark is coarse and quite unjustified!'

'Unjustified! After the sight of her in that gown last night! She concealed very little, and I am quite sure you did not object.'

'Annabel dresses fashionably, and it is not for you to criticise.'

'Then shall I dress fashionably, in a gown cut perilously low, and will you commend it?'

At this he lost his temper.

'I think it is time I reminded you of the terms of our marriage! This is precisely the sort of conversation I expect to be spared! If you remember, I am free to live my own life, and I'll have no nagging or criticism from you!'

'I was not criticising you, Harry. I am trying to understand your tastes, so that I may behave agreeably. So, I think I shall go bathing in the morning with Carbern, and wear a fashionable gown in the evening to dance with him.'

He had been gazing at her in the dressing mirror; now

he came over, seized her arm and pulled her round to face him.

'You will do no such thing! The Bath is a licence for all sorts of behaviour, and is frequented by such a lewd company as I do not intend you shall associate with!'

'Perhaps I should take that as a compliment. But let us be realistic. I am bound to associate with them *out* of The Bath.'

She could not resist goading him further, for his attitude was so unreasonable.

'Out of The Bath it may be unavoidable, but at least there is some chance of observing the proprieties. *In* The Bath, do you want men like Carbern putting their hands up under your bathgown and fumbling you? Did you not see what went on?'

She managed to take his remark with aplomb. 'Oh, I saw plenty of things, but no one seemed to object, so I thought I must be out of style . . .'

'Out of style or not, I expect you to behave with a certain amount of decorum!'

'While you go your own way? I thought we were *both* free to please ourselves.'

He was very angry; his eyes glared down at her.

'You have forgotten something. The most important part of the bargain—*your* part—is unfulfilled. *When I have an heir*—and not until then—you will be free to go your own way.'

'I have not forgotten. I have no chance to forget. Your mama spends most of her time watching me for signs, and now I must drink the waters to improve my fertility. It is provoking and most boring, and with your dancing attendance on Lady Annabel it is hardly surprising I turn to someone like Carbern for a little amusement.'

'I dance attendance!' He gripped her arm more

tightly. 'Do not be ridiculous! I warn you, do not give any favours to Carbern or his like. He is a man of bad reputation, and dangerous to a decent woman.'

'So you do not trust me to know how to behave?'

'Hell's teeth! Will you not see sense? You are not invulnerable! There are too many men here who take a delight in corrupting the innocent and perverting the good.'

'Oh, how amusing that will be! And I am not as innocent as I was—you have seen to that.'

He dropped her arm, caught her roughly and held her close to him. 'And I will go on seeing to it, by gad! If it's amusement you want, come to your husband for it! There's plenty I can teach you yet.'

Without warning he kissed her passionately, letting his mouth rove over hers, then passing over her face and throat, warm upon her cool skin, and then returning to her lips again. Against her will her being leapt and quivered, thrilling with excitement.

'It is no good pretending to be cold. I know you are not. And I am man enough for you.'

Katharine's colour was rising and her breath quickening. She was very near to betraying how she really felt. 'And you think that is all that matters?' she replied, as coolly as she could.

'It is all that matters to Carbern! He is interested only in your body—in making another conquest. It gives him more pleasure to seduce a decent woman than to take a whore, and he would debauch you without a second's hesitation.'

'But *you* are interested only in my body.'

'Damme, Kate, that's insulting! I am your husband . . .'

'Does that make it different?'

'Don't you know the difference? Do you think I'm like him? Don't you know me well enough to see that I care about you—enough not to want you to be hurt—and it's because of my responsibility for you that I am warning you!'

'That is something, I suppose.'

'Then remember this. I care not two straws what goes on in society. But I care what my wife does. So keep the bucks and bloods and lechers at a distance.'

'Was that part of our contract?'

'Damn the contract! Let this be a reason . . .' He took her in his arms again and kissed her fiercely. When he had finished, she laughed shakily and said,

'There's no reason in that. But as an argument it has some force—enough to make me remember . . .'

Afraid of betraying herself, she picked up her cloak and went downstairs to where the chairs waited to take her and Lady Cecily to the Pump Room.

Breedon, of course, went on horseback. In Bath everyone of consequence moved around the town on horseback or by chair, for the streets were narrow, dirty and crowded. Although Queen Square was fine and spacious, as were all the modern roads, such places were relatively few, and to get anywhere meant negotiating old streets, threading narrow alleys past mean buildings, in parts which one would not care to pass on foot for the filth—while at night there was the added danger of footpads. And yet, on reaching one's destination, such sordid ideas did not seem to exist. In the Pump Room, at the Assembly Rooms or on the Parades, one was surrounded by elegance and every evidence of fashionable society, and it was easy to forget there were parts of Bath where living was squalid and life was laborious, brutal and brief.

On the occasions when Katharine saw it at private parties, gambling fascinated her. Not the actual hazard of money—she despised people who could not resist a wager, who went on playing and losing and always hoping to recoup—but the fact that the players never seemed to see that in most games the odds were heavily against them; it was literally only the lucky ones who won. When she watched the gambling games she analysed them; most of them were pitifully simple, positively childish. How men could risk vast sums of money on the turn of a card or the throw of a boxful of dice was beyond her understanding. Playing for money on a game of skill was rational to her, for then you were backing your own ability. In watching and playing, Katharine relieved the boredom which set in for her once the novelty of the Bath social whirl wore off, and distracted her from the aching thought that Harry cared little for her except as a bed-mate and would soon leave her.

Several weeks passed, weeks of visits to the Pump Room by day and the Assembly Rooms by night, weeks of dancing and card-playing, in which visits to the theatre and to the concerts directed by Mr Herschel were pleasant diversions.

One morning Harry was stirring early, so Katharine rose as well, thinking she would breakfast with him since they were unlikely to be alone during the rest of the day. As they were filling their plates from the side table, she heard a light rattling of wheels, which stopped outside. He went to the window, and being curious, she joined him. Standing by the pavement in the care of a groom was the most elegant little two-wheeled chaise she had ever seen.

'What a beautiful little carriage! To whom, do you

think, does it belong?'

'It is mine,' Harry told her. 'My new chaise. I intend to try it this morning.'

It was then that she remembered overhearing a remark made by Annabel to Harry the previous evening as they were leaving the Rooms.

'Oh, Hawwy! An *open* chaise! The weather is gwowing cool—it might even wain! Lud, no!'

Katharine had thought nothing of it at the time, but now she realised that he had been inviting Annabel to drive with him. She hid her anger.

'How delightful that will be!' she remarked.

'You think so, Kate? Would you care to join me?'

'I should love to.'

'It is a cool, dull day. It may rain.'

'Then I shall take a cloak.'

And so, she thought, I shall profit by Annabel's refusal, and having breakfasted, they left at once.

'It really is most elegant!' she exclaimed, as they crossed the pavement.

It was the lightest thing she had seen, just a shallow body slung between two large wheels, with a low front and incurved back; the side panels were painted with a running design of vine-leaves, and the upper edges were carved into scrolls and arabesques, all heavily gilded. It was harnessed to a sleek horse little bigger than a pony.

'You like it?' Harry responded with the pleased smile of a satisfied owner. 'It is the very latest type of gig called a continental chaise—though it was built for me here in England. In spite of its looking so light, it is really quite strong. Come, will you mount?'

The step was little more than an iron ring set at an angle; Katharine carefully placed her foot within it, and Harry handed her to her seat. Then he got up beside her, took the reins from the groom and they were off

'Has Mr Spenlow seen this yet?' she asked.

'No. Why?'

'Because only yesterday he was praising your horses and carriages to me. In fact, he was teaching me a new language—bucks' slang! He said that your horses and vehicles are bang-up, and that you are a prime handler of the ribbons.'

'Did he, indeed! Well, I own, when I am on dry land I like to be well mounted. What else did he teach you?'

'Oh . . . that anyone venturing on foot in the outskirts of Bath at night would do well to carry a barking-iron or a cheese-toaster.'

'If you learn no worse than that, I shall not complain!'

As they were rattling over the grey cobbles, she thought, I have never seen the town like this before. It was far too early for fashionable society to be abroad; there was not a sedan chair or a carriage to be seen, only humble carts and barrows and drays, and the people they passed were the ordinary, necessary folk whose existence it was so easy to forget—the serving-maids cleaning area steps, the baker-boy with his basket of bread and rolls, a dairyman with his buckets, a knife-grinder, a chimneysweep.

They had left the fashionable streets around Queen Square, and were now in an older part in the centre of the town. As the gig turned a corner they saw an unexpected sight; a group of three men on foot—not working men; their brocade coats and cocked hats pro-claimed them to be men of fashion—and as they came nearer, Katharine's surprise increased. She recognised them as Carbern and two of his cronies, and saw that they were all considerably the worse for wear. Their coats were stained, their lace ruffles disarranged, their buckled shoes were filthy from the refuse of the streets. At first she thought they might have been attacked by footpads; then she saw that the stains on their clothes were not blood but wine, and the faces under the crooked hats and dishevelled wigs bore the signs not of blows but of drinking and dissipation. The three were walking, arms linked, supporting each other as they staggered along.

They looked up at the light tripping sound of the gig's wheels, and came on, Carbern lurching forward into their path. How repulsive he looks, she thought.

'Damme if it isn't Stonebridge and his handsome Kate, abroad so early in the morning!'

Harry acknowledged him coolly; she nodded.

'You're a queer fish, Stonebridge!' Carbern went on. 'Never seem to join the fun. I'll wager you spent last night in your own bed, a paragon of virtue—unlike us—the devil knows whose beds we were in!'

His bloodshot eyes leered over their pouched lids at Katharine.

'But they do say, virtue is its own reward. Never believed it meself. Yet, looking at pretty Kate—egad, I could think your night's work might have been better than mine—a lot cheaper, too.'

'Stand back, Carbern,' Harry retorted levelly, but there was a glint in his eye which made Carbern's companions draw him away from the side of the gig. 'Go home before you become too offensive,' he went on. 'Go and sleep off your night's amusement.'

With that, he slapped the reins and drove on.

Katharine hoped he would not notice that she was blushing.

'Now you have seen Carbern before his valet has been to work on him,' Harry remarked. 'He does not look so pretty after a night's gambling and whoring.'

'And drinking, too. They all look cup-shot.'

'I dare say they have a monstrous head apiece.'

'Whereas we have clear heads and a pleasant drive ahead! Where are we going, Harry?'

By this time they were driving down Southgate Street.

'I thought we would go in the direction of Bristol.'

'But isn't the way to Bristol at the crossroads below Milsom Street?'

'That is the London road. We are going on the lower Bristol road—it is not so busy and should be much more pleasant.'

They reached the bottom of Southgate Street, crossed the bridge and swung right. More houses, even meaner than those at the end of Southgate Street, were strung beside the road for some distance, and then quite suddenly there were no more buildings and they were driving along in sight of the river.

Katharine laughed. 'How unconventional we are! This has quite the air of an escapade!'

'I thought it would appeal to you. I cannot imagine what Mama will say when she misses us—but I promise you I will bear all her wrath. Shall I tell her I insisted on a second elopement?'

'Lud, no! The one was almost too much for her!'

The fields were flat and green on either side of the road, with here and there trees showing the first touches of gold and russet; there was little sign of population, just an odd cottage occasionally, and the traffic they passed was mostly late carts with produce going to market, and a few countryfolk on foot or riding rough-looking ponies. The elegant little gig provoked plenty of stares.

'I am sure your continental chaise is going to be quite a

sensation,' Katharine remarked. 'I can hardly wait to find out what choice phrase Mr Spenlow will find to praise it with.'

Harry chuckled. 'Some new piece of nonsense, no doubt! It pleases him to have all the latest slang on the tip of his tongue.'

'Yes, he pretends to great sophistication. But I think he is quite an inoffensive young man. He does a great deal of gambling, but that seems to be *de rigueur* in society. I am glad you do not gamble much – I have noticed that you prefer games of skill.'

'Oh, I gamble sometimes. I gambled on you. And I am beginning to think I did better than I expected. I find I enjoy your company, and can even tolerate your conversation.'

'Can you? But I cannot rattle away with gay trivialities, nor give you all the gossip, for I do not know any.'

'That is what I like about you. Gossip and flirtations are all very well, but sometimes one needs to have one's wits sharpened.'

'My wits will not remain very sharp, I fear! Harry, may I ask you a favour?'

'Certainly.'

'Could you arrange for me to join a lending library? I believe there are a number of them in Bath.'

'If that is what you wish, of course.'

The conversation turned on books, and they became so deep in talk that they were not aware that the sky was now positively threatening. They were in open country; Harry was keeping his eyes on the road ahead, for it was none too even and he needed to avoid the bigger ruts and pot-holes. A drop of rain splashed upon his hand.

'Gad, we are running into a rainstorm! What deuced

bad luck, when the weather has held until now.'

Katharine pulled her cloak about her, and retreated under its hood. 'Never mind. It may pass over.'

It did not. The rain began to fall steadily.

'We have not passed an inn for miles,' Harry remarked, 'and now there's not a house to be seen. Shall we go on or turn back?'

'Let us go on. There should be something ahead quite soon.'

She was in no mood for turning back; she wanted to have Harry to herself for as long as possible. But the road continued to be empty of any sort of habitation, and the rain increased. A breeze had sprung up which blew it into their faces, but she did not care—it was a good excuse to sit closer to Harry. After a while he looked down at her anxiously.

'My dear, you are getting very wet. I was a fool to bring you.'

'Not at all. The rain won't hurt me.'

He smiled. His head was very close to hers. 'It certainly cannot wash off your complexion! You have a lovely skin, Kate, and not a single pock-mark. I hate to think how much envy you must arouse.'

She darted him a bright glance.

'Oh, look, I do believe there are houses ahead.' He peered through the driving rain. 'I think you are right.'

There were houses: what was more, one of them was a tavern, small but decent-looking.

'Let us take our chance here, Kate.'

He dismounted. A young lad came out, goggle-eyed at the sight of such a smart turn-out. Harry handed over the reins, giving his instructions, and they hurried inside. A florid-faced man in an apron appeared.

Open your heart to Love
with 12 Romances Free
your welcome gift from Mills & Boon

Love, romance, intrigue...all are captured for you by Mills & Boon's top selling authors. By becoming a regular reader of Mills & Boon's romances you can enjoy twelve superb new titles every month plus a whole range of special benefits: your very own personal membership card, a free monthly newsletter packed with recipes, competitions, exclusive book offers and a monthly guide to the stars, plus extra bargain offers and big cash savings.

As a special introduction we will send you 12 exciting Mills & Boon Romances and an exclusive Mills & Boon Tote Bag FREE when you complete and return this card.

At the same time we will reserve a subscription to Mills & Boon Reader Service for you. Every month, you will receive twelve of the very latest novels by leading Romantic Fiction authors, delivered direct to your door. And they cost just the same as they would in the shops – postage and packing is always completely Free. There is no obligation or commitment – you can cancel your subscription at any time.

It's so easy! Send no money now – you don't even need a stamp. Just fill in and detach this card and send it off today.

plus the exclusive
Mills & Boon
TOTE BAG
FREE

FREE BOOKS CERTIFICATE

Dear Susan,

Your special Introductory offer of 12 free books is too good to miss. I understand they are mine to keep with the free Tote Bag.

Please also reserve a Reader Service Subscription for me. If I decide to subscribe, I shall, from the beginning of the month following my free parcel of books, receive 12 new books each month for £13.20, post and packing free. If I decide not to subscribe, I shall write to you within 10 days. The free books will be mine to keep, in any case.

I understand that I may cancel my subscription at any time simply by writing to you. I am over 18 years of age.

Name _____
(BLOCK CAPITALS PLEASE)
Address _____

_____ Signature _____

Postcode _____

2A6T

Remember, postcodes speed delivery. Our special offer applies in UK only and is not valid to present subscribers. Mills & Boon reserve the right to exercise discretion in granting membership. Should a price change become necessary you will be notified in advance. Offer expires 30th June 1986.

To Susan Welland
Mills & Boon
Reader Service
FREEPOST
P.O. Box 236
CROYDON
Surrey CR9 9EL.

SEND NO MONEY NOW

'We need shelter for ourselves and the horse – and a meal if you can manage it,' Harry told him.

'A meal, sir? I'll see what the mistress can do. Come you over by the fire.'

The room was small but clean, with two or three well-scrubbed tables and benches, a stone-flagged floor, and a wide hearth on which a log fire was burning. Harry took Katherine's wet cloak and draped it over a bench, and they stood by the blaze, grateful for its warmth, for the day had turned distinctly cold. Almost at once a plump cheerful woman appeared.

'Oh, sir—madam! This is a humble place, but you're welcome to what we have. Would you care for some mutton chops and boiled potatoes? That 'ud be hot —otherwise I can only give you cold beef and bread and cheese.'

'Mutton chops would be admirable,' Harry said. 'In the meantime, would some mulled ale be possible?'

'Of course, sir! Joe'll get that in no time! Now you and your lady try and dry yourselves off.'

The mulled ale was hot and comforting, and soon the potman came over to Harry. 'The mistress has laid your meal in the parlour, sir. There's a fire, and you'll be more private.'

Katharine picked up her still-damp cloak, and they followed him into a little room at the back. A newly kindled fire was burning bravely, and a small table set with a coarse white cloth and simple dishes was ready for their meal. From the look of the room with its lace curtains and cheap china ornaments, she guessed it to be the private parlour, and when the woman came in with a loaded dish, she said,

'It is very good of you to make us so comfortable.'

'Lor' bless you, ma'am, it's nothing! I hope this will be

to your liking. The horse has been seen to—you must stay until the rain gives over.'

The chops were well cooked; the two of them ate with relish, and the dish was followed by crusty new bread, a piece of good Cheddar cheese and a plate of apples. The rain still fell, and dripped off the eaves.

'Let us pull the settle round to the fire and sit there,' Katharine said, and they did so. She took another apple and sat munching, spreading her free hand to the blaze.

Harry leaned back and looked at her. 'What an excellent midshipman you would make, Kate. You take things as they come, and make the best of them.'

'I see no point in doing anything else. Complaining never made things any better!'

'I have made a thorough botch of things today,' he went on. 'I was so keen to try out the gig, and I wanted you to have a day you would enjoy—something different.'

'I have!' she said swiftly. 'The rain does not matter —in fact I am quite glad of it, for it is really cosy here, just the two of us in this little place. I think I prefer it to the Pump Room!'

She laughed up at him. He reached out and took her hand.

'Oh, Kate, you are quite splendid. Now I shall be able to remember this with pleasure, and not reproach myself too much.'

Her fingers were tingling, and her whole body seemed to respond to his touch. His expression was grave— tinged, she thought, with regret—and she looked at him with swift suspicion.

'Why are you talking of remembering today?'

'Why should I not?—Hell's teeth, I have got to tell you, so I may as well come out with it now, and plainly. I am recalled to my ship, Kate. I leave in ten days' time. And I have regrets, for I am well aware that my treatment of you could have been more—more considerate.'

For a moment she gazed at him in silence. It should be no surprise—she had been expecting it—yet now she knew it was inevitable, and imminent, the thought of his departure struck like a knife into her heart. She rallied herself.

'More considerate! Why, no, you have treated me well—better than many men treat their wives. I have nothing to complain of, so—you may go with an easy conscience.'

He gave her hand a squeeze, then released it and sat back without a word, his face still wearing that regretful look. Now is the time, she thought—I shall not have a better moment. She smiled at him encouragingly.

'I hope you will go with some satisfaction as well,' she said. 'You see, I am reasonably certain that I am expecting a child.'

CHAPTER
FIVE

HARRY'S EXPRESSION turned in a moment to surprise verging on incredulity.

'Expecting a child! Are you, Kate? Truly? Are you sure?'

Katharine laughed. 'You need not look so amazed, and act so dumbfounded! It is what you have been intending all along!'

'Egad, yes—but it is still surprising when it happens. I can hardly take it in! Why, then—when . . . ?'

'Oh, it is nearly seven months away. You will be on the high seas, I expect.'

'Damme, yes, so I shall.'

'So it has turned out very conveniently. It will be settled before you go, and by the time you return, the child should be past the howling stage.'

'I must say you are taking it very coolly!'

'Probably because I haven't the least idea about it.'

'You shall have the best doctor—Mama will see to that. Great heavens—you are pregnant and I have allowed you to get soaking wet! If you catch a chill, it will be my fault!'

'I shall not catch a chill. And I do not propose to tell your mama for at least another week, when I am more sure of it.'

'By which time she may have forgotten the soaking!

Well, well! And a little while ago you were complaining of not having enough to think about!'

'Oh, Harry, I am not going to sit and concentrate on my pregnancy like a broody hen!'

In spite of himself, he had to laugh. 'What a picture that conjures up! No, I suppose not. But—afterwards —you will not hand him over entirely to a nurse?'

'Indeed, no. I see no point in having a child and then being a stranger to it.'

'I am glad. I hardly knew my mother until I was ten years old.'

The rain became a light drizzle, but the skies showed no sign of clearing, and Harry reluctantly agreed with Katharine that they might as well set off. There was one thing to be grateful for—her cloak was now reasonably dry.

They talked little on the way home; Harry had a slightly bemused air, and seemed preoccupied with his own thoughts and the business of keeping the horse from stepping in pot-holes which were now treacherously filled with rainwater so that their depth could not be judged. The little chaise bumped and swayed along, thick brown mud spurting from its wheels, the sound of the horse's hoofs muffled in the mire. The rain drizzled monotonously, and they were both getting very wet again. But they were together; even the silence was companionable.

Katharine in her heart was happy that she was going to give Harry something he wanted; and he, she supposed, besides being bemused was happy, too, that he stood an even chance of having an heir. Had he possibly considered that the baby might be a girl? Perhaps she had better not think of that, either: if she thought hard enough of it as a boy perhaps it would be so!

They were on the outskirts of Bath, and there was still very little traffic. Pedestrians were few; those who had to be abroad were muffled up and walking head down into the drifting rain as if they could not get out of it soon enough. She admitted to herself that she had had enough of driving for the day; she, too, would be glad to be indoors before a good fire. Idly she scanned the road ahead, and the few walkers, who would cower into the side of the road as they passed. Harry, she had been glad to see, was more considerate than most drivers; he slackened speed and tried to give them a wide berth, unlike most of the bloods who rattled past regardless of anything and sprayed people on foot with sheets of liquid mud.

Katharine's casual glance fixed on the figure of a woman ahead; there was something vaguely familiar about her. How could there be? Everyone looked the same, swaddled up against wind and rain. And yet . . . The gig slowed a little, drew out, came abreast, and passed.

She slewed round in her seat, put her hand on her husband's arm and cried, 'Harry! Please stop!'

He reined in the horse. The woman plodded on towards them, and on hearing that they had stopped, she looked up.

'It is!' Katharine exclaimed. 'It's Mrs Partridge!'

The woman's face softened in sudden recognition. 'Miss Katharine!'

'It's my father's old housekeeper,' she said quickly to Harry, then turned back to look at her.

'Mrs Partridge! What are you doing here?'

'I'm living in Bath with my brother, Miss Katharine.'

And not doing too well, Katharine thought: she looked years older, she was thinner, her face more lined, her eyes tired and anxious.

'And what do you do?' she asked.

'Very little, more's the pity. Work is hard to get—at present, just a little sewing . . .'

'I am sorry the gig is too small for us to take you up. Do you have far to go?'

'Not very far, Miss Katharine. And I'm used to walking now.'

'Come and see me as soon as you can. I am sure I shall have some sewing for you. Ask for me at Lord Embercombe's house in Queen Square. This—this is my husband, Viscount Stonebridge.'

Standing there in the mud and rain, Mrs Partridge did not neglect to bob a curtsy. 'Your servant, m'lord! So it's true, Miss Katharine?'

'Yes! But now we must all get out of the rain! I shall hope to see you.'

Mrs Partridge smiled, and the gig drove on.

'Thank you for waiting, Harry,' Katharine said. 'She is such a good woman—I must see what I can do for her. I think she has not been faring too well,'

'Then you must certainly find some work for her.'

As soon as they were inside the Queen Square house, Harry was calling for Katharine's maid and giving orders for a fire to be lit in their room.

'And I should like a large tub of hot water,' Katharine added. 'I intend to take a hot bath.'

It was blissful after being cold and damp to be sitting in steaming water in front of a crackling fire. It was raining more heavily again, slanting in lines of fine silver across the window panes, dripping from the gutters and splashing from the sills, but that made her bedroom all the cosier. Betty wrapped her mistress in a huge towel as she stepped from the tub, and began to rub her dry. They were thus engaged when the inner door from the dressing-room opened, and Harry appeared. He had rubbed down and changed, and was wearing just his blue evening breeches and a white ruffled shirt.

'How do you feel, Kate?' he asked, with a hint of anxiety.

'Splendid!'

'You do not think you have caught cold?'

'I am sure I have not. The hot tub was wonderfully comforting. Thank you, Betty, I can manage now.'

As the maid left the room, Harry took Katharine, towel-swathed, into his arms, and his eyes as he gazed down at her held a look she had not seen before. It was serious, tender, concerned; almost, she thought, loving. But that couldn't be—if it were so, then it was for the baby, not for her.

'I wish I did not have to go,' he said.

'But you must. Do not worry—I shall not do anything foolish!'

'Egad, no! You must take care.'

His hand touched her hair, which being only loosely pinned began to tumble down; he stroked and fondled it, twining it in his fingers.

'Such hair, soft and shining—and how sweet and fresh you smell.' His hand slid under the towel to rest on her shoulder. 'And your skin is so fine and smooth.'

He bent and very gently kissed her lips. In some strange way it was more exciting than if he had kissed her with obvious passion.

'I shall remember you like this when I am at sea. Soft and warm and sweet-smelling—my dear little Kate.'

'You—You should not call me such a thing—you do not mean it,' she whispered.

'Of course I mean it! You little goose, do you not

realise that you have become quite dear to me, in your own odd way, in the past few weeks?'

'How could I know? I thought—you put up with me—simply because you wanted an heir.'

'It was not as simple as that! I admit I married you on impulse, but do you think I would want a son by *any* woman? You do yourself less than justice.'

Again he gave her that gentle, tender smile. Katharine felt her throat tightening, her heart giving little fluttering beats. Naked within the folds of the towel she felt her body tingling with awakened desire, yearning and very vulnerable. She wanted Harry so much —but oh, if only she did not always feel she was to him a second best.

'I own I have a fondness for you, Kate—as you, I hope, have for me,' he went on.

'It's true—I have.'

He lifted her chin with one hand, still holding her close within the circle of his arm. 'I am glad to hear it. I'd not like to think you made love with me so joyously only with the body, and felt nothing else.'

Joyously—that was a kind expression for him to use about her passionate response. Suddenly abashed, she turned her face and leant her head against his so that he could not see her blushes.

'And I . . .' he added, '*I* did not make love only to get a son.'

Now she turned to him smiling, lifted one arm and put it around his neck. 'That makes it so much better, Harry.'

The towel began to slip from her shoulders.

'Yes, I shall remember you like this—soft and warm, sweet-smelling and beautiful,' he murmured.

'*Beautiful?*'

'Don't you know you are lovely? And I am glad to hear you do not find me as disagreeable as before.'

'Disagreeable! Oh, Harry, I can be happier with you than with anyone . . .'

'Then our marriage is turning out well, even though at first neither of us cared for the other, and each suited our own ends.'

Then, mouth to mouth, there were no more words, only those spoken in her heart. Please God, let the voyage be a short one, and send him home soon . . .

The next ten days passed swiftly; there was so much to do. They returned to Embercombe, where Harry's packing must be completed, and there Katharine decided it was time to tell his parents the news of her pregnancy.

Lady Cecily, while graciously approving, conveyed the impression that she had merely achieved what was expected of her, and put her at once in the wrong over the matter of timing.

'You should have mentioned the possibility when we were still in Bath, then you could have been examined by someone of established reputation.'

'I am quite satisfied that I must be pregnant.'

Lord Embercombe broke in, as usual not mincing his words. 'Well, Harry, that's a load off me mind. The gal is capable of breeding. Now we must see if she could carry and bear a healthy boy. We don't want a string of gals.'

The Embercombe brood mare, Katharine thought.

Any hopes she had cherished of having the baby at Embercombe were swiftly dashed. Lady Cecily announced that soon after Harry's departure they would go to London, and there they would stay until after the birth.

'Travelling will become increasingly inadvisable, and

in London we will have the pick of the best doctors.'

'I beg you will choose carefully, Mama,' Harry replied.

'Harry, you may trust me to make a good choice.'

'Perhaps, Mama, you would consider my friend John Anson.'

'I have never heard of him! It is not likely that he has sufficient status.'

So the suggestion was dismissed out of hand; but when they were alone, Katharine asked Harry about his friend.

'He is in practice in London, and also attends one of the lying-in hospitals. He is young, but experienced.'

'Then please give me his address. And there is one other thing I should be glad if you would do for me.'

'Anything!'

'It is this. You remember we met my father's one-time housekeeper in Bath, and I gave her some sewing to do?'

'Yes?'

'She was too proud to tell me, but I am sure she is living in want. There are so many people in Bath who cannot get work, and I feel certain there is not enough money coming into her brother's house to keep his family. I should so like her to work for me. Now that I am expecting the baby, she could be very useful. None of the other maids needs to be displaced.'

'Since you like her and want her, I shall most certainly arrange it.'

So a servant was sent to Bath with a letter from Katharine to Mrs Partridge, and a generous sum of money for travelling, should she decide to come. He returned with her grateful acceptance, to be followed a few days later by Mrs Partridge herself. Katharine felt comforted. When Harry goes, I shall still have an ally, she told herself; she can be a kind of lady's maid and companion.

Besides her other talents, Mrs Partridge knew how to glean information, and she soon brought Katharine news of Sir Joshua.

'They do say he is not so well, Miss Katharine. And Walcotte is going to rack and ruin.'

'That does not surprise me,' she answered drily. 'He always left the management to that rascally bailiff, who no doubt is busy cheating him right and left.'

'There is no bailiff now, m'lady. Sir Richard Stukely seems to have taken over with *his* bailiff, but they do precious little. The tale goes that Sir Joshua has sold a lot of his land to Sir Richard.'

Handed over to cover gambling debts, thought Kate, since I could not be bartered.

'So my father and Sir Richard are still friends?'

'Sir Richard is always at Walcotte. Even Mrs Cusson has been heard to say that he encourages Sir Joshua to drink and gamble too much.'

'I can well believe it.'

The day of Harry's departure arrived—the hour, the moment, when he was bidding her goodbye. Seeing her moved, Harry, held her and kissed her, then cradled her head on his shoulder and murmured,

'Don't grieve, Kate. The time will pass, you will have the baby to think of—and you will write to me often, won't you?'

'Of course! And you must tell me everything you are doing.'

'I shall. Then we shall each have a fine packet of letters to read when a mail-ship gets in. And, Kate, do not forget to tell me how you are feeling—with the baby . . .'

'I shall probably bore you with my sensations! Oh, we

still haven't settled the baby's name!'

'Mama will insist on one of the family names, so you will have little choice, I fear.'

'But if it is a girl?'

'Then you may call her anything you please.'

She threw her arms round his neck. 'Harry, I shall miss you so much . . .'

'Kate, dear, do you think I shall not miss you? But all sailors and their wives have to endure this—please God it will not be a long voyage.'

'Thank heaven we are at peace. I shall not have to worry about your ship being in action.'

'There, you are looking on the bright side already! Now, I must go. Goodbye, dear Kate.'

He kissed her again. She blinked away her tears and gave him what she hoped was a confident smile.

'The time will soon pass,' she said firmly. 'And then we can all be together—all three of us.'

And what is going to happen in the meantime? she wondered, gazing at his retreating figure. Now I am left to be ruled by his parents, and even the baby seems unreal at present. I suppose I shall learn to get used to it; it is not so uncommon a situation for a girl to be in.

But she wished with all her heart that Harry had not gone back to sea.

The months passed. As Lady Cecily had intended, they had gone to London and there they had stayed, in the Embercombes' large and comfortable town house just off Piccadilly. The social life was very similar to that in Bath, except that they went to fewer public places and more private houses; and apart from reading, Katharine's only distraction was cards, at which she now had considerable practice.

She wrote long letters to Harry, trying not to let him see how bored she was, recounting incidents she thought might amuse him. At first it was like writing to herself, nothing more; it was three months before any letters came from him.

Lady Cecily began to read hers; a few moments later, she exclaimed, 'Great heavens!' and collapsed back in her chair.

'What is wrong?' Katharine asked quickly, trying to ignore the sympathetic jumping of her own heart.

'Do you not see!' Lady Cecily fumbled for her vinaigrette. 'God's mercy, it could hardly be worse!'

'What?' Katharine pressed in alarm.

'Harry's ship—it is posted—to the West Indies!'

'That is a long way away, of course—but—but we are not at war . . .'

'What an ignorant girl you are! Do you not know what a posting to the West Indies means? The death-rate is enormous!'

Katharine stared at her in stupefied silence. Lady Cecily sniffed at her vinaigrette.

'My poor Harry! My poor, poor Harry!'

'But—*why?*'

'Because of the fever! They nearly all catch it—they die like flies!'

Katharine tried to rally her.

'Surely it cannot be as bad as that? We would have no Navy left.'

'Why do you think the press gangs are always busy? I tell you, it is dreadful—dreadful! The officers suffer as much as the men.'

When Lady Cecily said, 'I fear the worst. Thank heaven we have at least the chance of an heir,' Katharine decided that it was all a ridiculous exaggeration.

Lady Cecily had engaged her favourite doctor, a gentleman named Pomeroy who had a fashionable practice. Katherine, who had been prepared to tolerate him, soon found her feelings turning to active dislike. His stock phrase seemed to be, 'Good or ill, Nature has her way in the end', which, even when preceded by 'We help as best we can', appeared to her a good excuse for any failure on his part to bring the balance of nature down on the side of good. His air of bonhomie did not convince her that he had great knowledge or skill; she would have liked better evidence, such as successful treatments. Even Lord Embercombe's ailments, which seemed to be centred on his liver, had apparently derived more benefit from the Bath waters than from anything Pomeroy had done. But he and Lady Cecily were convinced there was no better man—which does not say much for the rest, Katharine thought.

It was not her nature to be passive, and now she felt she had good reason to seek out Harry's friend John Anson, for careful conversation with some of the men of her acquaintance made her think there could be some grounds for Lady Cecily's fears for her son. Dr Anson, she found, was a man of Harry's age; slim, soberly dressed and quiet of manner, yet giving an impression of underlying confidence and capability. As soon as formal introductions were over, she asked the question which had been disturbing her.

'You are Harry's friend, and a doctor. He is posted to the West Indies, and may by now be there. I should like you to tell me honestly what danger there is to health for him?'

His answer to her question was not what she wanted to hear. There was danger, he admitted it: fevers were rife, little was known about their cause or treatment; they

were serious, and a severe hazard. But Harry was
healthy, he added, and his way of life not given to excess;
he could be relied on to take such precautions as were
known to be advisable.

'Now, as to yourself, Lady Katherine, are you well?'

'Yes, I thank you. I only wish I had been allowed a
doctor of my own choice.'

'I imagine your mother-in-law made the arrangements?'

He is no fool, she thought.

'Yes. She engaged Dr Pomeroy.'

'He has . . . a considerable reputation.'

'Of what sort?' she retorted caustically. 'If good, it
seems somewhat unfounded. He does not inspire my
confidence.'

The young doctor tried not to look embarrassed. 'He
is—a little old-fashioned, perhaps, but he is thought to
be one of the best doctors. As to his methods for
childbirth, I know nothing of them.'

'I wish . . . I wish I could feel . . .' She was groping for
words. 'In an emergency, would you attend me?'

Dr Anson looked surprised. 'Professional etiquette
being what it is, Lady Katherine, I could not take over
his case behind his back, you know that.'

'Yes, I know. But . . .'

He smiled reassuringly. 'I understand. It is natural to
be a little nervous over a first pregnancy.' Then his look
became serious. 'In a real emergency, Lady Katherine,
if asked I would of course give a second opinion. But do
not worry; basically, childbirth is a natural thing.'

And with that she had to be content. She hoped her
nervousness was not a premonition, and that Nature in
having her way would behave as she should.

*   *   *

Katharine lay on the bed, pain washing over her. How long would it be? An hour or so yet, Mrs Partridge had said. At first no more than twinges, spaced well out, now the pains were strong and frequent, each surging up like a great wave beating through her, so that she had to breathe hard and grip the mattress with either hand, holding tight until the ebb set in, and slowly her body was free again. It was late evening and the doctor had been sent for; she could only wait and ride each successive pain and pray that the baby would not take too long about its arrival.

She was gripped by a spasm of pain longer and more violent than ever. Gritting her teeth, she thought that Nature was certainly having her way, and it was not an easy one. She grunted, panted, gripped the mattress until her hands ached.

Mrs Partridge bent over her. 'Is it bad, Miss Katharine?'

She nodded. 'How much more? Where is that confounded doctor . . .?'

'He should be here any minute. Try to be easy, my dear.'

Easy! That was the last thing she could be. And she knew the doctor should have arrived an hour ago. Should it be as long and as painful as this? She had no way of knowing—her first baby, and probably her last . . . *How long?*

There were footsteps on the stairs. The door opened, and Dr Pomeroy's voice, full of condescending good humour, addressed her, wafted on wine-laden breath.

'Well, well, m'lady, and how do you find yourself?'

What a foolish question!

'That is for you to say.'

'The pains are frequent?'

Gripped in a violent spasm she could only nod.

'Good. Then it is all going well.'

He lifted the bedclothes, gave a cursory glance at the grossly distended belly bulging out her nightdress and said, 'Nature will have her way.'

If he says that once more, I shall scream, she thought.

'I shall return in a few minutes,' he said. 'Lady Cecily awaits my report.'

Katharine had seen his flushed face bending over her; his eyes were full, bloodshot, pouchy; his breath smelt heavily of wine. The good humour was a mask; beneath it was a man who was irritated by having to hurry a good dinner, who did not feel like bestirring himself and who now intended to drink brandy with the Embercombes and let her fend for herself until the last minute. Just how much did he know about delivering babies, she wondered.

. . . Oh, God . . . the pain . . . Should it be as bad as this with nothing happening? She could not even ask, for he had gone.

How much later it was when he returned she did not know; it was to her a pain-filled eternity. His red-veined jowly face came and went above her, and she heard not only his voice but those of her parents-in-law.

'How is she?'—That was Lady Cecily.

'Making rough weather of it?'—That was Lord Embercombe.

'No change. Mother Nature is taking her time.'

Katharine could not stifle a scream at a fresh wave of pain, then lay back panting.

'Birdie . . . Birdie . . .' she whispered, using Mrs Partridge's old pet name.

'I'm here, my dear.'

'I must speak—to his lordship . . .'

'What is it, m'gal?'

'Please send—for Harry's friend—Dr Anson . . .'

'Eh? Harry's friend? What's the gal after?'

'Please—I must see him!'

It was difficult even to think through the mists of pain, but she knew something was wrong, and she must appeal to him, for Lady Cecily would never agree . . .

'Dr Anson—Birdie knows where . . .'

'What d'ye say, Pomeroy?'

'Quite unnecessary! That young upstart! Full of new-fangled notions . . .'

'Well, the old-fangled ones don't seem to be getting far.'

'Please, m'lord!' That was Birdie's voice, low and anxious. 'She's very weak—you don't want the child to be . . .'

'Another opinion won't hurt. Send for him.'

'If he intervenes, I shall not be responsible.'—That was Pomeroy.

You're not responsible now, she thought, you're a drunken, ignorant, conceited fool—then everything once more gave way to pain.

'Hold on to me, Miss Katharine. Don't mind gripping when the pain's bad.'

It was bad all the time. It went on and on. She tried to think of something else, but it was impossible, she could not even conjure Harry's face out of the mists that surged around her. She lay there, grasping Mrs Partridge's hand, clawing at the mattress, biting her lips, gasping, giving panting cries and feeling herself growing weaker as the pain kept rending at her body. She was bathed with sweat; Mrs Partridge dabbed her brow with a damp cloth, held a glass of water for her to sip in the brief intervals between the waves of agony.

And so it went on: there was no time, no thought now, only pain. Dr Pomeroy seemed to have gone away—to drink some more brandy, she supposed.

The door opened, and closed again.

'How is she?'

It was Dr Anson's voice, quiet, calm, sober.

Hazily Katharine saw Anson's profile as he bent down, young, pale, professionally calm.

'She needs help, at once,' he said. 'Don't worry, Lady Katharine, we shall manage between us. I shall need you, too, ma'am—I know you are in great pain, but try not to fight it, that only makes it worse. Cry out if you wish, it sometimes helps. It is a large baby, and a somewhat awkward young creature. Just try to do as I tell you.'

His manner, his very presence, gave her confidence. Before, she had been thinking, the baby will never come—it will die—we shall both die. But now there was someone here who knew what to do. It made all the difference. For Harry's sake—for her own sake—she wouldn't give up, she would do what he told her— she . . .

'That's right. That's good. Not much longer . . .'

Now she had to cry out; she could not contain the pain within herself. And that will bring Pomeroy, she thought.

'I—won't—have—Pomeroy—here!' she gasped between her teeth.

'Forget him, Lady Katharine. Just do as I tell you.'

It was fine for men—they wanted sons—they should have the bearing of them—God, what an easy time men had—but this man, at least, was doing what he could.

Anson continued his work.

'Fine, Lady Katharine. It goes well.'

One more great agony.

'There now—the rest will be easier.'

Again . . .

'That's right . . .'

Again—would it never come? Then, with incredible swiftness, she felt a slithering rush, and her body shed its burden, became relaxed and empty—no more pain —and she heard a cry.

'Mrs Partridge—hold the child there.'

A pause, and then another cry, hard and strong, and another—

'Lady Katharine, you have a big, healthy boy.'

She lay back, hardly conscious, aware only of a wonderful sense of physical relief and mental triumph. She had done it! Harry had a son.

All too soon, Lady Cecily invaded her room again. 'Well, that is a good thing over,' she announced, as if it were she who had given birth. 'I have sent for the wet-nurse.'

Katharine, feeling slightly light-headed after the strain, threw caution to the winds.

'Then you may send her back again,' she replied. 'I intend to feed the baby myself.'

'To feed . . .! You can do no such thing! It is unthinkable—only common women feed their babies!'

Katharine thought of a wet-nurse she had seen in a house in Bath—a blowsy, sluttish-looking woman. Perhaps they were not all like that, but she had decided that no strange woman was going to put her baby to the breast if it could be avoided.

'Your Dr Pomeroy is always talking about Nature having her way—that is what is going to happen. It is most natural for a mother to feed her child.'

Dr Anson had approved when she had suggested it, and said he considered it better for child and mother, provided the mother was in good health.

'It is quite barbarous! I shall not allow it!'

'Lady Cecily, this matter is personal to me, and I intend to feed my baby.'

There was a pause; Lady Cecily was taking stock of the situation. 'Very well, if you are set on it, you may try it. You will soon find it such a troublesome business that you will be glad to behave with the decorum appropriate to your position.'

On looking back, Katharine realised that it was this defiance, and the supplanting of Pomeroy, which turned her mother-in-law's attitude from dislike to active enmity. Before, she had been cold and disapproving; but her behaviour had been neutral. Now she adopted a pleasant manner—for had not Katharine produced a son?—but this was a mask for a well-thought-out campaign of spite. It was a little while before she could believe this, and then she thought, why does she hate me so? I have done exactly what was wanted—given birth to a son within the year. Perhaps that was a twisted kind of reason. A girl baby, while proving she was fertile, would still have meant failure, and she could then be blamed and pitied; enmity would be unnecessary. Success, coupled with defiance, gave grounds for hatred where dislike already existed.

Feeding the baby herself, of which Lady Cecily so disapproved, gave broad grounds for her campaign. Katharine found she was virtually a prisoner in the house—whenever visits were being paid, they always coincided with feeding times.

'If you must feed the child, you must do it in the privacy of your own nursery. I cannot have it known that the baby has no wet-nurse.'

So even when they were going to private houses where Katharine could have taken the baby and retired to feed him, she was usually left at home, and said to be in a delicate condition; and to go out to public entertainments, Lady Cecily said, was quite impossible. If she wanted a short drive, there was always some reason why the small carriage was not available. She found that only by appealing to Lord Embercombe when he was alone could she get the carriage for long enough to take a turn round the park, accompanied by Mrs Partridge. If people had not come visiting, she would have had no society at all.

Meanwhile, thank heaven, little Edward continued to thrive, and was to her a never-ending source of wonder and delight. It was strange that a baby—which she had privately considered a rather boring and exacting scrap of humanity—should be, when it was your own, such a fascinating, lovable creature.

Harry had not forgotten their bargain. A few days after Edward's birth was announced, she had received a letter from the lawyer telling her that the sum they had agreed upon was hers outright, and available to her whenever she wished. How furious Lady Cecily would be if she knew, Katharine thought. She would call it being handsomely paid for doing no more than her duty.

In her letters to Harry, she had been as tactful as possible; she had not mentioned that Pomeroy was drunk and quite unable to assist at the difficult birth; she had merely written that she had had to call on Dr Anson at the last minute, and all had gone well. No point in telling him her agonies; the baby was healthy and thriving, that was all that mattered.

It became increasingly difficult to write to him; there

was so little to tell once she had given a report of
Edward's progress. She was far too proud to complain to
him of his mother's behaviour. No, there was simply
nothing to write about; she went nowhere, and her
supply of books had strangely diminished.

'No doubt you have read everything suitable,' Lady
Cecily said when she remarked on it. 'I trust the lending
library knows better than to send you *Merryland* or some
other of that kind.' She had named a flagrantly porno-
graphic book which for some time had been enjoying a
great success.

'I think I would welcome even that!' Katharine said on
impulse, and instantly regretted it. Now she will tell
Harry that I require the library to send me lewd books,
that the evil side of my character is developing in his
absence.

So her letters, still full of loving messages, enquiries
about Harry's health, his life, his diversions if any,
nevertheless became shorter and shorter.

It was a tremendous relief to her when it was
announced that the family would go to Somerset for a
spell. Embercombe or Bath—wherever it was, life must
be better than in London. Christmas was past; Lord
Embercombe was looking forward to some hunting.
Katharine was sure she would not be allowed to ride to
hounds, for Lady Cecily had not even permitted her to
trot in Rotten Row.

'When you are feeding the child! Impossible! You'd
have no milk!'

It was impossible to argue about it, as well.

It was Mrs Partridge who found out, three days after
their arrival, that Sir Joshua Walcotte had died only the
day before; and shortly afterwards a lawyer's letter came
for Katharine. It told her that, apart from a few small

legacies, the whole of her father's estate had been left to 'my old friend Richard Stukely, who has stood by me through everything'. There was nothing for her. The lawyer added that her father's chief creditor was the same Richard Stukely, who also held the mortgage on Walcotte Grange and owned a large part of the land. No wonder he had 'stood by'!

Katharine did not know how Mrs Partridge got her information. Walcotte was some distance from Embercombe, yet she managed to keep in touch with all the news and gossip. When one of Lord Embercombe's grooms was dismissed for ill-treating a horse, it was Mrs Partridge who knew that a groom from Walcotte was in need of a place. Katharine knew him well from her childhood; a small, lean man, always busy, who said little, but what he did say was shrewd and to the point. She had expected that he would now be working for Stukely, but it seemed that he was not. Mrs Partridge told her he had been offered a job, and had refused it. Now he was paying for his independence—jobs were hard to come by.

'Tell him to apply here,' Katharine said. 'I'll have a word with Lord Embercombe's bailiff. I know John Hobley is a good man.'

And so, with her recommendation and the bailiff's assessment, Hobley got the post as groom. When he saw her, he was quick to thank her.

'I doubt whether I'd have got the job without you, m'lady—there were several others after it.'

'I know you're a good worker, and reliable, Hobley, and I said so. You are here on your own merits.'

'Still, I thank you, m'lady.'

'And I haven't forgotten that you taught me to ride.'

His face creased into a smile. 'Excuse me, m'lady. I
have something which should be yours.'

Mystified, she watched him disappear into the stable
and come out with a parcel carefully wrapped in clean
sacking. When she removed this she found a picture
—the portrait of her mother.

'John! How wonderful! How did you get it?'

'Let's say I found it, m'lady. I didn't think it would be
missed.'

'I cannot thank you enough!'

They looked at each other like conspirators. She had a
feeling that she now had two allies at Embercombe.

But they were allies who at this stage could not help
her. Katharine had to fight her battles on her own—and
she usually lost. Lady Cecily was dominating the nursery
more and more, dictating how Edward should be
clothed and cared for; fussing over him, having him
brought from his cot to be displayed to visitors even
when he had just fallen asleep. Protests fell on deaf ears,
Lady Cecily went her own way, and the nursemaids were
too much in awe of her to go against her orders. That was
not surprising; it was Lady Cecily who engaged them,
and she could dismiss them at will. What can I do?
Katharine wondered. When Edward is a little older, he
will be disastrously spoiled and my efforts at discipline
will be set aside. Already I hardly count; I am simply the
woman who feeds him. The thought that she could be
replaced as easily as one of the maids was not a pleasant
one.

At last a letter came from Harry, saying that he had
just received the news of the baby's arrival.

I am thankful that all is well. It is a sobering thought,
to be father of a son one has not seen. I pray the time

will not be too long before I am with you both.
Meanwhile, take good care of him, Kate, and of
yourself. You do not say why Anson was called, but I
know you could not have been in better hands. I am
sorry Mama thinks that Pomeroy was overridden in a
high-handed manner; I do not see why you or Anson
should do that. I dare say it is all over and forgotten by
now . . .'

It was to be expected that Lady Cecily would have
made some complaint to Harry. Katharine refused to let
herself be troubled by it, especially as he was dismissing
it as being over and done with. She would have been
much more concerned if she had known that Lady
Cecily's letters to him were full of twisted information,
all of which subtly put Katharine in a bad light. It was not
until he received a letter from Anson telling him some
details about the confinement that Harry himself began
to wonder whether his mother's letters might not be
somewhat biased.

Just as Katharine had thought that things must be better
when they moved from London to Embercombe, so she
thought they might improve when they went from
Embercombe to Bath. There, there were outside distractions, more time was spent out of the house, and
with the ready availability of sedan chairs and only short
distances to travel, it must be possible for her to have
more society. Although as it turned out she was not as
free as she had hoped, it was better; and she had the
great pleasure of renewing her friendship with Sophia
Spenlow. Sophia came calling as soon as she heard that
Katharine was in Bath; she was delighted to see her
again and was enchanted with little Edward.

'How wonderful for you, Katharine, to be a mother! And how Harry must be longing to return to you both! Is there any news of an end to his posting?'

'Not yet. And he has been gone over a year.'

Katharine did not complain to Sophia of her mother-in-law, but Sophia was not a fool. She spent time alone with her, which other guests did not, and she was soon observant of Lady Cecily's interference in nursery matters and the way her enforced desires frequently ran counter to Katharine's wishes. The other private annoyances and humiliations she did not see, but she could tell from the change in Katharine's appearance and manner that something was gravely wrong. At last she made gentle enquiries, and Katharine told her enough to leave her appalled.

'But it seems there is nothing I can do about it, so I must put up with it until Harry comes home,' she added.

'Oh, Kate, I am so sorry. How extraordinary that she should be so spiteful!'

'She always resented the marriage, that is the reason. Harry should have married an heiress, and one of their choosing.'

'But now that you have given her a grandson, she should be reconciled.'

'Perhaps she cannot forgive me for that, either.'

CHAPTER
SIX

WEEKS PASSED with Kate becoming desperate for news of Harry. She felt that before long he should be returning to England, but she had no hint of it, and all the time her life was growing more difficult. Lady Cecily's attitude was often almost unbearable. She dominated the nursery, which she invaded at all hours, and if Kate gave an instruction, it was sure to be contradicted. Kate could keep no routine for Edward; she had to stand by and see him being mismanaged and spoilt. But that was only part of it.

Now Lady Cecily insisted on the social round. Kate could not understand her change of attitude, and found the socialising as trying as her previous seclusion. The people that Lady Cecily entertained were not the type that she found at all interesting to be with; the women were empty-headed scandalmongers, the men unintelligent, downright stupid, gamblers and lechers. And, strangely, Lord Carbern, who had been unpopular with Lady Cecily, was now encouraged to visit them.

Whenever possible he pressed his attentions on Kate. Lady Cecily now seemed to think him agreeable and amusing, and allowed him to come when other visitors were not expected. And so it happened that one day Lady Cecily excused herself from the drawing-room, and Kate was left alone with him. He lost no time in profiting from this, and had seated himself at the other end of the sofa which Kate was occupying; now he leaned back and looked at her appraisingly.

'Well, Lady Kate,' he said, 'you make an attractive grass widow. It is time you had some consolation.'

She understood perfectly what he meant. 'I neither need nor want any,' she replied firmly.

'Come, come, little Kate, you must be practical. Think of your situation! As a wife you have not seen your husband for—how long?—certainly more than a year, and since he persists in this ridiculous notion of being a naval officer you are likely to go on seeing precious little of him. Such men stay home only long enough to get their wives pregnant and then are off again. They rely on that to keep their wives out of mischief. So they cannot complain if their wives seek a little distraction.'

'I do not need distraction!' she said forcibly.

'Your constancy does you credit, my dear. But such a bewitching creature cannot go without a man for long. We cannot allow it! Why cannot we come to an understanding? Let me be your consoler—your protector. There would be pleasure in it for both of us. And for you there would be the added advantage that I would keep your other suitors at bay.'

She was fascinated by the sheer audacity of his lechery. She could hardly believe her ears. He was actually proposing that she should be his mistress! She looked at him in cold anger.

'Lord Carbern, your proposal is not only unwelcome, it disgusts me. I trust you will have the good sense not to repeat it.'

Getting to her feet, she found she was trembling.

'Faith, Kate, I'll swear you look devilish handsome

when you are angry. Too handsome for me to give up the chase.'

She heard his mocking laugh as she marched from the room. He had not laid a finger on her, yet she was shaking with revulsion. The way he looked at her had stripped her. At all costs, she decided, she must prevent a repetition of the incident.

At the first opportunity, she spoke to her mother-in-law. 'Lady Cecily, I pray you will not in future leave me alone with Lord Carbern.'

Lady Cecily raised her eybrows. 'And why not, may I ask?'

'Because the last time you did so, he asked me to become his mistress.'

'You must have misunderstood him.' Lady Cecily regarded her coldly. 'Sometimes, Katharine, I think your imagination runs away with you. I am sure he was only offering you a little distraction. Most young women would be overjoyed to be singled out for Lord Carbern's attention.'

With this Kate had to let the matter drop. It was plain that she was getting nowhere. And since Lady Cecily made no attempt to protect her from any future advances, she herself took every precaution not to lay herself open to them. But she could not help being puzzled, and the next time she was able to have a private chat with Sophia Spenlow, she told her all about it.

'What I cannot understand,' she said at last, 'is Lady Cecily's attitude. You would think the last thing she would want was for her son's wife to be preyed on by someone like Carbern. Yet she pretends it isn't happenings; she does nothing to stop it; and for all I know, she encourages him.'

Sophia looked serious and thoughtful. 'She has never liked you, I know.'

'No. And now I think she positively hates me, though why, I cannot imagine.'

'It is my belief that she wants to get rid of you.'

'Get rid . . .? Well, I suppose it could be so. But surely, for the family's reputation, she would not want me to become Carbern's mistress!'

'I am not so sure.' Sophia, though quiet, was surprisingly shrewd. 'Have you thought what the situation could be when Harry returns?'

'What do you mean?'

'When Harry comes back, if you are Carbern's mistress, she will certainly be rid of you. Harry would not take you back.'

Kate felt herself grow cold. She had not thought as far ahead as that. Harry would not be complaisant; he would not want her if she had given her favours elsewhere.

'Even the suspicion of it might be enough,' Sophia added.

'Enough for her to make trouble! Yes, she is quite capable of that.' Then another idea struck her. 'But she is making one mistake—a big one! What about Edward? They want an heir. But if they drove me out, I would take him. He is my baby, and they would lose control of him. She can't risk that.'

Sophia leaned forward to clasp her hand. 'Oh, my dear, you are still underestimating her. That is all part of it. Do you know that, if you were to commit adultery, or even be suspected of it, that would be quite enough in law for Edward, in Harry's absence, to be taken from you and given to them.'

Cold horror was followed by an equally cold rage. So

that was Lady Cecily's game! She intended to get rid of
her, and keep Edward. And when Harry came back, she
would say, 'See how she behaved in your absence! You
are better off without her—and you have your son. I saw
to that.'

'Sophia, the woman is a fiend! What can I do?'

'Just what you have been doing, dear. Keep the
men—all men—at a distance. Do not give her a chance
to blacken your character.'

'Yes, I see that. But you cannot know what it is like at
home—I cannot be happy even with Edward, for she
rules the nursery, she constantly spoils him and over-
rules me. I have no authority at all.'

'Poor Kate! It must be dreadful for you. But you must
stand firm and pray for Harry's return. Everything will
be different then.'

If only Harry would return. At times Kate thought, I
can't go on much longer. Now, when she went out with
Lady Cecily in public, that was no pleasure. Wherever
she appeared there was some member of the rakish set
who would do his best to importune her. There were
young bloods, Carbern's disciples, always ready to cluster round, toasting her in their glasses of brandy, scan-
ning her from head to toe, making lecherous remarks
while peering down her bodice.

And women are supposed to enjoy this! she thought in
fierce revulsion. We are expected to be flattered by it!
They consider that for a man to want a woman's body for
the use of his lust is the greatest compliment he can pay
her. And there are actually women like Lady Cecily who
appear to agree with it! Whether she does think so or
not, she makes no attempt to save me from it.

One night Kate could not contain her resentment. 'Do
we not know any respectable men in Bath?' she ex-

claimed. 'I might almost be a whore from the way they treat me!'

Lady Cecily replied with a calm close to insolence. 'Are you really so naïve? Your husband is abroad, and yet you go out and about. Of course the men think you are in the market, ready to go to the highest bidder.'

'But *you* take me out! And it's not true—they could not all be so stupid! They must know I love Harry.'

'Perhaps they think that is a pretence, as it may well be. Behaving as you do, you are well placed to find out who would make the most generous protector.'

'I do not want anyone but Harry! It should not be necessary for me to die of boredom indoors to prove my case!'

'Necessary or not, some might think it so.'

Kate choked back her rage, told herself this vicious woman could not represent decent opinion, and resolved more than ever not to give in. When Lady Cecily insisted on taking her out, she went, and braved the men's behaviour by always keeping women's company.

All this Kate could have borne if she had any respite at home, but at last she knew she would have to take action or she would be broken, and the only action she could take was a desperate measure indeed. The more she thought of it, the more desperate it became—and the more attractive. The difficulty lay in how to achieve it. It would take much planning, some luck—and money. The last, praise God, and thanks to Harry, she possessed.

She tried to think of a way round the practical details. As yet, she did not dare to confide in Mrs Partridge, for she believed one of the nursery-maids observed their private conversations and took everything she heard back to Lady Cecily. She could not be too careful. She must wait. Meanwhile, she decided that at nine months, Edward should be weaned.

In this she did manage to secure Mrs Partridge's help. Without her it would not have been possible: nine months was early for weaning, and if Lady Cecily had heard of her plans she would have immediately engaged a wet-nurse and thwarted them. But Edward was a healthy child with a lusty appetite, and with Mrs Partridge's collaboration she was able to make it appear that she was only supplementing the breast-feeds. By the time Lady Cecily found out what was going on, Edward was virtually weaned, and she had to accept it. Another black mark against me, Kate thought. I wonder if she will find another way to spite me?

She did. Lady Cecily's reaction was to take her out, night after night, and keep her from home later than ever. At the assemblies in Harrison's Rooms she would say to everyone, 'Katharine considers herself quite free in Harry's absence, and demands distraction. I put my feelings aside and accompany her—and I am sure I can rely on you to keep her amused.'

Lord Carbern was ever present, with his gloating eyes and rapacious smile. One night he said suavely, 'I am at Lady Kate's service any time. Now, Lady Kate, I propose that you allow me to escort you to the races on Lansdown—a party of us are going.'

'Thank you, Lord Carbern, but no.'

'But if you want distraction, you *must* come to the races!'

He moved closer, standing so that his bulk cut her off from the rest of the group. 'How can I make my offer more attractive?'

He paused, but she did not answer, so he went on,

bending to murmur in her ear, so that amid the noise and chatter of the crowd no one else would hear.

'It is not fair! You are so devilish bewitching, and you are playing us all one against the other. After so long, you must need a man. Go home after the races, and I shall send a chair for you. Then we shall have supper in my rooms—a supper brightened for you by a diamond brooch—and followed by some delightful dalliance—and no one need hear of it.'

She clutched her fan tightly, to stop herself from striking him across the face with it. In society, such approaches were accepted as compliments; if one did not want to take up the suggestions, one laughed them off. But it was not easy for her to swallow what she considered an insult.

'Lord Carbern, I must disappoint you once again.'

She had spoken out loud; to cover his chagrin, he appealed to the rest of the group.

'We all know Lady Kate is virtuous, but do you not think she must be an angel? She never requires the company of our sex! But angels have been known to fall, and I shall still hope for that. Now, I suppose, she will consider me a demon incarnate! Am I right, Lady Kate?'

A roar of laughter swept up, and she knew that it was at her expense, she was the only virtuous one in their loose company. She was blushing, but her voice rang out crisp and clear.

'Well, sir, you may not be a demon. But I think Hell must be empty, since Bath is now so full.'

This time the laughter was in support of her sally; they could appreciate it, although it was against themselves. Only Lord Carbern eyed her with a look more calculating than amused.

*   *   *

The opportunity for which Kate was waiting came in an unexpected form. One morning a message arrived from Sophia, saying that she was unwell and would welcome a visit from her. Wondering what was wrong—because the previous evening she had seemed perfectly well —Kate left with Mrs Partridge as soon as she could. When they arrived at the house that Herbert Spenlow had rented for the season, they were shown upstairs to the drawing-room, and to Kate's surprise Sophia was there, not in bed in her room as she had expected. But something was very wrong. Sophia did not look ill, but was sitting sunk in abject misery, her face blotched, her eyelids swollen, trying to stem the tears which still flowed into a quite inadequate handkerchief.

Kate ran over and knelt down beside her.

'Sophia! You are not ill—you are dreadfully upset! What has happened?'

'I don't know how to tell you—it is too awful! Oh, Kate . . .' Sophia suppressed a sob. 'I must tell you—no doubt it will be all over Bath by nightfall . . . It is my brother . . .'

'What about him? Not injured?—a *duel*?'

'No, not that. He—he went gaming last night—all night—he only returned a couple of hours ago . . .'

'And?'

'And—he has lost all our money!'

'Great heavens! The fool! But never mind, Sophia. I shall give you enough so that you will not need to leave Bath just yet.'

'You don't understand, Kate. I do not mean that he has lost the money for our stay in Bath. He has lost it *all*—our entire fortune—his, mine and, I believe, what should be my mother's!'

In one night! Kate had heard of such things among

men who gambled for high stakes, but had thought such
tales must be wildly exaggerated. It was not conceivable
to her that anyone could be so foolish, so reckless. Yet
here was Sophia, telling her that young Spenlow had
gambled away their complete livelihood.

'It cannot be as bad as that,' she responded. 'Something must remain—estates, lands that bring in rents
—you will have something left . . .'

Having told the grim truth to someone, Sophia
seemed to have reached the stage of numbed acceptance. 'He pledged our property, too. I really do not
know how I shall manage to live. There is the dower
house which my mother has—he did not stake that—I
do not know what else—practically nothing.'

'It cannot be as bad as you think.'

'I fear it is! But until he confronts my mother with the
truth of it, we shall not know.'

Kate was now seething inwardly with fury. How could
men have the power to do this sort of thing? They might
ruin their own lives if they chose—that was their affair
—but wantonly to ruin women who were dependent on
them, all for the excitement of the turn of a card, the roll
of dice—it was a monstrous injustice that only the rule of
men could perpetuate. Women had no voice, no power.
They merely suffered—and would no doubt scrape and
pinch so that their men, their rulers, should not go
without. It sickened her simply to consider women's
impotence.

'Who won the money?' she asked at last.

'Does it matter? There were several at the start.
Gradually, it seems, they dropped out. Herbert had
already lost quite heavily, and Carbern kept challenging
him. Giving him the chance to win back his stakes,
Herbert said. But of course he did not win, and each

time he lost he put the stakes higher. On the last throw, Carbern won everything.'

Spenlow the fool, and Carbern the knave—what a combination!

'I hope Carbern meets a bullet one day.'

'Kate, that is a dreadful thing to say!'

'I mean it. He has shot more than one man in a duel, I hear. I have no doubt he will go to Hell, but he'll not suffer there. He will be enjoying himself at the Devil's high table.' For Sophia's sake, she must be practical. 'My dear, what are your plans?'

'Plans? I have none. I cannot bring my mind to bear on the disaster yet.'

She put her arms round Sophia, stroked and rocked her like a child, while her brain leapt into action, taking stock of the whole situation.

'The rent is paid on this house?' she asked.

'Only until the end of this week. Herbert was hiring it by the month. Of course we must leave.'

'Where will you go?'

'Back to my mother, I suppose. I do not feel I can face the journey back to Gloucester yet, but neither can I face the thought of cheap lodgings here.'

'No. But your brother must certainly go and tell your mother what he has done. Now, Sophia, may I make a suggestion?'

'Please do. Anything!'

'You may think that I am turning your misfortune to my own advantage, and in a way I am, but I think it may help both of us. Sophia—Birdie, I am going to surprise you. Birdie, I have had no chance to tell you what has been in my mind for some time.'

'What is it, Miss Kate?'

'Just this. You both know what my life with the

Embercombes is like. I have decided I cannot stand it any longer, I must leave.'

'*Leave?*' Sophia's eyes were wide with horror. 'But how could you?'

'I have made plans, but I could do nothing about them while I am in Queen Square, for I am constantly spied on, as the maids listen to our conversations. Now, if I rent a house, will you come and live with me for the time being, Sophia? You cannot possibly stay anywhere by yourself, but the two of us could chaperon each other, and you would come too, wouldn't you, Birdie? It would tide you over until you know enough to make permanent arrangements. What do you say?'

'Why, I should love to live with you, Kate—but surely it is impossible?'

'Not if we act now. You, Birdie, will have to make all the arrangements about hiring the house.'

'But, Miss Kate, it needs money!'

'That I have—from my husband—and the Embercombes cannot touch it. Now, when I go home, I shall leave you here, Birdie, to look after Sophia for a few hours. But in fact you must go and look for a house. It should not be too difficult to find something suitable; there is quite a lot of furnished property to rent just now. If you are unlucky, you must do the same tomorrow, and I shall say I am sending you to Sophia again. What is it, Sophia?'

'Kate, there is Edward—what . . .?'

'Edward is coming with me, of course. That is an important part of it. And that is where Birdie and I shall have to be very clever, to get our things packed up without the maids noticing, and prepared enough for us to get ourselves, Edward and the trunks out of the house when both the Embercombes are absent. If my mother-in-law finds out beforehand, she will do everything to stop me. I cannot tell you when we will be coming; we must pray for an opportunity before the end of the week. As soon as I am installed, you can move from here to join me. What do you think? Will you agree?'

'Agree? Gladly! But I do not see how you can possibly manage it.'

'You must leave that to me and Birdie.'

After a discussion in which Kate arranged a number of finer points with Mrs Partridge, a chair was called for and Kate returned to Queen Square.

They agreed to tell the truth about Sophia's situation. It could not be concealed for long, so when Lady Cecily said to Kate, 'And what is wrong with Miss Spenlow? She is a sickly creature,' Kate replied, 'She is not ill, but very upset. That feather-witted brother of hers has lost all their money at the tables.'

'Is that all? They can send home for more—and tonight he may have a run of winning.'

'He has lost so heavily that there may be no reserves. That is why she is so distracted. I think I must send Mrs Partridge to her tomorrow.'

'If you feel inclined to mollycoddle her, that is your affair.'

The first part of the plan went well. Mrs Partridge found a suitable house in Miles's Buildings, and a banker's order covered the initial payment. It was the escape from Queen Square that presented all the difficulties. It was far worse than an elopement, Kate decided. For that one could travel light; but for this she must take most of the wardrobe she had brought to Bath, as well as everything needed for Edward's immediate care, and baby things, although small, were very numerous. All this had to be in a sufficient state of readiness so that, when the

Embercombes went out without Kate—whenever that might be—Mrs Partridge could hurry out to tell the carter, previously warned, that they needed him at once, and on his arrival they could pack and send off the luggage, themselves following by chair before the Embercombes returned.

But Lady Cecily's new tactic of taking Kate everywhere with her threatened to defeat all her plans. Kate was reluctant to plead illness or a headache, for her mother-in-law was quite suspicious enough to send her own maid to sit with her. The weekend was almost upon them, and Kate was getting desperate when fortune once more played into her hands. The Embercombes had an unexpected invitation to dine with an old friend passing through Bath; he was a judge, and she had not met him. Lady Cecily decided that Kate must stay at home; and Kate was sure it was sheer perversity, for at the dinner-table there could be the intelligent conversation she so desired. But now she had no regrets when the Embercombes dressed and left in their carriage without her.

It was by the greatest effort of will that she kept her composure after sending Mrs Partridge out to alert the carrier. Suppose he had had a rush of work, and instead of keeping a cart waiting he had sent the last one out and gambled on having one back when she needed it? Suppose, for some unforeseen reason, the Embercombes returned? Those were the two worst possibilities, and were enough to keep her on tenterhooks.

Mrs Partridge came back, and shortly after, the carter arrived. Kate and she had hurried about, collecting and packing, and were soon ready. Then Kate put on her most confident and authoritative manner, and the trunks were carried downstairs to a background of whispered speculation on the part of the Embercombe servants, but no one dared to ask what was going on.

Kate had written the briefest of notes: 'My life has become intolerable here. I am leaving, and taking my son with me.' She signed it, put it on Lady Cecily's dressing-table, and returned to the nursery.

Edward was awake, and crowed with delight when she picked him up. The carter had moved off; two chairs were at the door. At first the servants had thought that only Mrs Partridge was leaving, but then they had seen Edward's paraphernalia being loaded with the trunks and had realised what was happening. Now they unashamedly stood around watching, whispering to each other, their faces showing a range of emotions from simply curiosity, through surprise, amazement, to total stupefaction.

Kate's nerves were at full stretch, but at last she was beginning to feel success within her grasp. Literally, for Edward, a warm, wriggling, gurgling bundle was safe in her arms; she held him close, not wanting to surrender him even to Birdie in this hour of daring and triumph, as she went downstairs into the hall. She looked at the group of servants clustered in the rear, and did not speak. She did not know if any of them were sympathetic, so why should she trouble?

Mrs Partridge held Edward as Kate got into the chair, then placed him in her arms again. The door was shut; there was a lurch as the chairmen took the load—and she was off, moving at walking pace out of Queen Square and, she hoped, out of the Embercombes' lives. At last she was independent—and free!

CHAPTER
SEVEN

It was a long time since Kate had had a letter from Harry. The last one she knew by heart. It was brief, for which he apologised, saying they were at anchor off-shore and that there was a great deal of fever, 'for which I can do very little, and it is taking its toll'. He did not say that he had caught it, but she feared it, for his writing was irregular, though that might be due to haste.

I long to see you again, but there is no word yet of our sailing. Sweet Kate, at such distance you are still close to the heart of your affectionate husband, Harry.

It was the nearest thing to a love-letter that he had written, and she prayed it was not also a farewell.

Her escape had gone smoothly. From Queen Square to Miles's Building was no distance—one simply went up Gay Street, turned right into George Street, and the next turning on the left was Miles's Buildings—but to Kate it might have been a hundred leagues, she was so completely out of the Embercombes' orbit.

Queen Square was fashionable, Miles's Buildings was respectable; the Queen Square house was large, this one was smaller, but adequate for her simple household. Queen Square was usually thronged with carriages and riders. Miles's Buildings was quiet; the houses, with only

the front steps and the railings enclosing the basement
area standing between them and the pavement, looked
across the narrow street to a stone wall which ran at
more than head height along the lower ends of the back
gardens of Gay Street, to which wooden doors at regular
intervals gave access. The simplicity and seclusion suited
Kate admirably, and when Sophia arrived, bringing
her maid and her cook, the new household settled in.
Herbert Spenlow had gone to Gloucestershire alone; it
was only fair that he should take the burden of giving his
mother the shocking news.

Sophia and Kate revelled in the novelty of their life
together. Sophia became an honorary aunt; and Kate,
with Mrs Partridge to guide her where necessary, was
able to care for Edward in all the many ways that had
been taken out of her hands in Queen Square. For about
a week their existence seemed the nearest thing to
heaven; but then the idyll was abruptly broken, not by
the return of Herbert with Sophia's financial worries,
but by the arrival of a stranger.

He requested to see Kate, and gave the name of
Harrington. She had never heard of him, and was at
once suspicious, so she sent the maid to enquire his business. Back came the reply: he was a lawyer. Knowing
nothing more, she thought it best to admit him.

He came in, a stout man in late middle age, with sharp
eyes and a rat-trap mouth. He bowed to the three
women, his look sweeping over them.

'The Viscountess Stonebridge?' he asked.

Katharine nodded.

'My business is on behalf of the Earl of Embercombe,
and is private, m'lady.'

Sophia at once rose, but Kate laid a restraining hand
on Mrs Partridge's arm, and said to the lawyer, 'I require

my companion as witness and chaperon.'

At the mention of Lord Embercombe, Kate had felt a
warning shiver. Harrington opened the door for Sophia
and closed it behind her, then took the seat Kate
indicated.

'And what is your business, Mr Harrington?'

'I come with a request from Lord Embercombe that
you and your son return immediately to live under his
roof.'

She had steeled herself for this, but still felt a qualm of
unease. But she spoke as firmly as before.

'That is impossible.'

The lawyer's voice was smooth as silk. 'Not *impossible*, Lady Katharine. You may be unwilling, but I trust
you will overcome your reluctance and give me an
assurance that you will return.'

She looked at him proudly. 'No, I will not return.'

He was quite unruffled, his tone of voice unchanged.

'Then I am sorry, m'lady. Your refusal has been
provided for, and I am obliged to give you this.'

He brought out a document from an inside pocket.
She did not attempt to take it, so he placed it on the
sofa-table beside her.

'What is it, Mr Harrington?'

'It is a magistrate's order, m'lady, requiring you to
return the Honourable Edward Breedon to his grandfather.'

Her heart gave a sickening lurch. He can't do that, she
thought, I've done nothing wrong.

'Edward is my child, and he stays with me.'

A cruel gleam flashed momentarily into Harrington's
eyes.

'Forgive me, m'lady, but the Honourable Edward
is your child only by accident of birth—biologically

speaking, you might say. He belongs in law to his father.'

'His father is overseas, as you well know.'

'Indeed, yes. In that case, all legal rights devolve on the father's family—in other words, Lord Embercombe now has all rights over the child, and you must surrender him.'

'*Surrender* him! You must be out of your mind to think I will give up my child!'

One stubby forefinger reached out and tapped the document.

'M'lady, you have no alternative.'

To her surprise he got up, went to the door, opened it and beckoned someone inside.

A burly, thickset man, respectably but humbly dressed, with a face low-browed and square-jawed and an expression both dour and determined, came to stand just inside the room.

'This is Wilson,' Harrington said, and dismissed him with a nod. His voice now sounded positively in-gratiating.

'Now that you have seen Wilson I think you will understand. It is his job to put this order into effect. In other words, if you refuse, he personally will take the Honourable Edward and return him to his grandfather.'

Kate stared at him, speechless with horror. It could not be true—such a thing could not really happen! That man—would he actually snatch her baby from her, and take him by force back to Queen Square, in spite of anything she could do?

'I cannot believe it,' she whispered.

'Indeed you must believe it, Lady Katharine. Wilson is a strong man; I do not know what servants you keep, but he can summon help if necessary. Should you resist, it would be a most distasteful incident, and fraught with terror for the child. But Wilson has his duty to perform, and a household of women with their servants would not stop him.

With his steely eyes still fixed on her, he went on, 'We do not wish to do that. We wish to escort you, m'lady, and your child, peaceably back to your rightful home in Queen Square.'

Kate did not answer. She sat, rigid with revulsion and horror, trying to understand the situation, and to find a way out of it. These men—she had no strength to defeat them. All she had were her wits.

'If . . .' she said at last. 'If I agree to go back, you will give me time—time to pack my things, and the baby's?'

'Of course, m'lady. You shall have an hour—that should be enough.'

How should she manage in an hour? But she must . . .

'Yes, an hour. You have servants to do your packing. A carriage will be sent for you. In the meantime, Wilson will remain here so that he can keep his charge under observation.'

Her heart sank. That was her last hope gone. She felt sick and exhausted. They had thought of everything —that she would try to slip out of the house with Edward and hide somewhere—even that desperate action was to be denied her. Wilson would be watching Edward. At the first sign of any intention to take him away, that great brute of a man would snatch her baby. No, there was nothing she could do. For the time being, the Embercombes had won.

Since she must give in, she would do so with dignity. This lawyer, who positively enjoyed playing Lady Cecily's dirty games, should not have the satisfaction of seeing her screaming and crying, shouting protests or having hysterics.

'I shall be ready in an hour,' she said.

Sophia was horrified, but agreed that Kate had no alternative.

'But I am not beaten, Sophia. I shall keep in touch with you. I won't give in to them.'

An hour later, Kate, preceded by her trunks and carrying Edward in her arms, went out with Mrs Partridge to the waiting carriage. When they entered the Queen Square house Lady Cecily came out of the drawing-room. Her eyes were gleaming and there was a thin smile of triumph on her lips.

'So you have seen reason,' she said.

Reason! What reason was there in a magistrate's order and brute force? Kate did not answer.

'I have come to inform you of our new arrangements,' Lady Cecily said. 'In Harry's absence, all rights over Edward pass to his grandfather. He, and I, consider that you are not a fit person to have charge of our grandson. You will now confine your visits to the nursery to half an hour each day. The head nurse holds the key of the nursery. She will see that our wishes are enforced.'

With that information, Lady Cecily left.

When Kate went to kiss Edward good night, the nursery door was locked, and remained so in spite of her calling and knocking. Defeated and fighting back her tears, she went to her room and spent a sleepless night turning the situation over in her mind. The next day she came to a decision. Edward, her baby—she could consider him completely lost to her. The time the Ember-combes were prepared to grant her would do no good to either of them. He was inexpressibly dear to her, but she must adapt to life without him. She had now no husband

and no child. With Mrs Partridge's help, she packed her belongings and left for a second time—but now she had to go without Edward.

At Miles's Buildings she took stock of her position and reckoned up her probable living expenses. There were matters to be settled. One of these was the question of servants, and Mrs Partridge came forward with a valuable suggestion.

'Miss Kate, we are a household of women; and for some things, that doesn't do. We need at least one manservant. John Hobley approached me on the quiet when we were moving out, and said he would like to go with us. He would much rather work for you than stay with Lord Embercombe.'

'But, Birdie, I do not know if I need a full-time groom, or if it would be wise for me to afford one, for that means horses, and of course a carriage. I like Hobley—I wish I could employ him, but . . .'

'That will be all right, Miss Kate. He's not sticking out for a post as groom. He'll come to you and work in any place you like—manservant, footman, anything you like to say.'

Oh, good John Hobley! Outwardly the most un-emotional of men, he had such a strong streak of loyalty, he was so honest, so absolutely trustworthy, that he would be a treasure.

'He's not bothered about wages, Miss Kate.'

'No, Birdie, he shall have ten pounds a year, and he'll be worth every penny. I shall be most grateful for his services.'

The other matter was less easily settled. She knew her mind would never be at ease until she was quite convinced that she could do nothing to get Edward back. There might be a possibility of contesting the magistrate's order; she could perhaps fight the case, and have the decision reversed. She must find out. There were lawyers a-plenty in Bath, and Sophia was knowledgeable, and told her the name of one with a good reputation.

Under the name of 'Mrs Brown', she made an appointment to see Mr Dewley. At the office she took the chair he placed for her and said, 'I must admit to you, Mr Dewley, that my name is not Brown. I thought that if you knew my identity in advance it might— unintentionally, I am sure—influence the advice you may give me.'

He inclined his head, giving her a shrewd glance. He may already have guessed at my position in life, she thought, but he does not know who I am.

'As you wish, madam. I appreciate your honesty. What is the matter about which you wish to consult me?'

As lawyers went, thought Kate, he was fairly prepossessing. He was a very plain man with heavy features, but there was a certain humanity, even a touch of humour, in the expression of his brown eyes, and his mouth was firm without too much hardness.

'Briefly, this is the situation.'

Kate summoned her confidence and plunged into her story.

'I am married, but my husband is overseas, and I am unable to contact him. I have one child—a little boy, just under a year old. If . . . If my husband were to die, my child would be his paternal grandfather's heir. They —my parents-in-law—have always been very possessive of the child, and unfriendly to me, for my husband married me against their wishes. Recently their attitude became so antagonistic that I left their house, taking my child with me.'

Dewley sat, making a steeple of his fingertips, and nodded. 'And then?' he prompted.

'They obtained a magistrate's order as guardians of my child, and compelled me to take him back to them. Once we were in the house I was cut off completely from the nursery, and I was told I would not be allowed to see my baby except for one half-hour each day. I could not bear it. I left the house again, alone. What I want to know is this—can I contest the magistrate's order, and get my baby back?'

For a moment he did not speak. Then, 'What reason was given for keeping the child from you?'

'That I was unsuitable to have care of him.'

'You say you left the house for the second time. Have you returned there?'

'No. Such conditions would be torture.'

'You have no——friends—to whom they might object?'

Kate looked him full in the eye. 'If you mean, have I a lover—no.'

'Forgive me, I have to know all the facts. Well, Mrs Brown, without hearing any more details I can only make an arbitrary judgment, but I do not think fuller knowledge would alter my opinion in the slightest.'

She looked at him in sudden hope. He seemed sympathetic; surely he could help her?

'My advice to you is; Make peace with the child's grandparents, and go back. If you are conciliatory, their attitude may soften.'

'*Go back!*' She was aghast and angry. 'Is that all you can tell me? Can I not contest the order?'

'Of course you may. You are perfectly free to do that, but I can offer you no hope of success. In the absence of your husband, his father is the legal guardian.'

'I am the child's mother! There can be no closer bond

than that. I love him—and though he is so small he must miss me. How is it possible in common humanity for him to be kept from me?'

'Legally he is not being kept from you, unsatisfactory though it is. And in spite of being his mother, in law you have no claim on him. That rests in his father and his father's family. And you have aggravated the situation by leaving—technically you have deserted the child.'

'Deserted . . .! They forced me back with him, and then—my life there is deliberate torture!'

'The fact remains that you have no claim to him. It would be foolish to embark on litigation which you have no chance of winning.'

'Mr Dewley, I am the Viscountess Stonebridge. I can afford a lawsuit.'

He did not blink an eye, or alter the tone of his voice.

'My lady, if you go elsewhere, you may easily find a lawyer to take your case. Some cannot resist the temptation of high fees. But, I am telling you, you may take years and spend a fortune, you may petition the House of Lords, but the result will be the same. There is no precedent that will take the custody of the child from its grandparents and give it back to you. Custody is in the male line. Spend what you will, it will be to no purpose.'

Kate was stunned. It was so much worse than she had feared! Dewley seemed an honest man, and against his own interests he was giving her no hope at all.

She came out of her trance to find him standing beside her.

'A glass of wine, my lady. I think you need it.'

Kate was a fighter. She took the blow, and as soon as she had absorbed the shock of it she set her mind to thinking of other plans. Brooding was useless; she had already discovered how soul-destroying that was. She needed action, something to exercise her brain in another direction. And she was seething with a contained anger. Just as she had rebelled against her father's intention to force her into an unwelcome marriage, so she leapt into revolt against the Embercombes' assumption of all rights over her child. This was the law of the land! A law which treated a woman's bonds with the child she had borne as nothing, so that men could ride roughshod over their womenfolk. And why not—men made the law! She had always thought it grossly unjust that men had such power, but only now was she feeling the full force of it. Women had no more rights than animals.

But she, Kate Breedon, was not going to lie down and be trampled on by men. There must be some way of striking back, and she would find it. Plainly it would have to be a subtle one.

When the idea first came to her, she was dazzled by it. Yet her first reaction was that it was not possible. But the idea did not go away, and she found herself considering it first from one angle and then from another. And she began to say to herself: It needs three things—money, planning, and audacity. I have money, I have the ability to plan—and what I have suffered has made me ready to dare anything. If I could only do it, how superb it would be! It would be a sweet revenge on the dominance of men—and a few personal scores might be paid off, too.

It would be illegal—but why should I care about that? I hate the law—and I'd willingly risk a fine for the pleasure it would give me. Sophia would be shocked to the core, but she would understand. So would Birdie. And there was John Hobley; she felt at once that he could become her right-hand man in such a venture.

The time was right, the place was right. Bath was

ready and ripe for the opening of a place of pleasure such
as she envisaged. A private gambling club, to which men
could come only by invitation; a select few, high players,
who would keep their mouths shut rather than risk
having such an attractive place closed down. Men who
would win and lose from each other, but who by the
inevitability of gambling would lose to the 'bank' which
the club would run; men who would be amazed to find
the club was ruled by a woman.

Everything must be right. There must be no
loopholes, no weak points in the structure. And from
every angle, secrecy was vitally important.

She needed another house. The more she thought
about it, the more she realised that it must be one with
easy access from Miles's Buildings, for she would have to
go to and fro late at night. Then, as if Fate at last had
decided to smile on her, she found the perfect one. It was
in Gay Street; upper class, fashionable, just a shade
down from the luxury of Queen Square. And the door to
the back garden of the house in Gay Street across the
narrow road of Miles's Buildings was almost opposite
her own front door.

Mrs Partridge had negotiated the lease of Miles's
Buildings, so she must not be seen to be in any way
connected with a proposed lease in Gay Street. Hobley
would have to do that—and in fairness to all, he, Birdie,
and Sophia must be taken into her confidence. So she
held what she called a council of war.

When the first wave of shock and incredulity had died
down after the announcement of her proposal, she
began one by one to kill off their objections.

'No one will know my identity. I shall always go
masked—the men will find that intriguing.'

'The club will not be generally known. I shall start by

inviting a nucleus of heavy gamblers to join a private club. I shall make it most attractive to them, and they will know they must keep it secret, or the law may intervene.'

'Technically it will be a succession of private parties, and as such, outside the law. So no one will be admitted unless he is a member, there at my personal invitation.'

'Quarrels and fights? I shall not allow them—they will be nipped in the bud. As in the Assembly Rooms, gentlemen will not be allowed in wearing swords. They will be able to buy food and drink, but anyone showing signs of getting drunk and quarrelsome will be asked to leave—and the men will see the wisdom of keeping the club a quiet and respectable place.'

'I shall engage some men—Hobley will find them for me, won't you, John?—who are capable of helping to run the tables and tough enough to take a firm line.'

'How will it pay? Well, of course, they will be gambling against each other in some of the games, but in others there is a bank—and in the long run, the bank always wins. *We* shall always hold the bank. And of course there will be a high subscription to join the club, and the food and wine will not be cheap.'

'Yes, I have thought of a name. I shall call it— "Hell".'

Katharine planned everything in minutest detail. As soon as the lease was hers for the Gay Street house, she inspected it closely. Until then she had been relying on Hobley's account of it. Whenever she went there, she entered under cover of darkness, crossing the road to the garden door, for no one must ever guess that the respectable Viscountess Stonebridge leased another house where fashionable bloods might come and go.

When Kate and Mrs Partridge went shopping, she

would take a mental note of things to her taste for furnishing, and Hobley would be sent to order them. He found this venture much to his taste, and soon proved himself invaluable. He supervised the workmen who had to be called in to get the house in order; he acquired the stock of cards and dice they would need; he bought the gaming tables; he engaged a male cook, a kitchen boy, a waiter and several men capable of running the games of chance. When the men were engaged, Hobley had to get clothes for them; they were to be dressed alike, and Kate had planned everything to heighten the atmosphere she intended to create.

Hobley also bought Kate a small carriage and a horse, and took them to Embercombe, on an errand for her. He was instructed to collect all the clothes she had left behind there. This was not meanness on her part; in her new role she must have clothes that would not be recognised as her own; and since costumiers were notorious gossips, she did not want to have new ones made. At Embercombe there were garments she had never worn. Meanwhile, she spent hours compiling a list of men she should invite to be members of Hell, and drafting a letter which would be irresistibly attractive without incriminating her.

With everything arranged to her satisfaction, the hired men were assembled, to be rigorously drilled and rehearsed by herself and Hobley. For this she was masked; not even the servants should know her identity; they were a tight-lipped bunch, but there was no point in risking an inadvertent betrayal.

A date was fixed; the letters drafted and dispatched. Now came the worst part—with plans completed, and everything ready, she had to wait. To wait, like a fisherman dangling a tempting bait into a promising pool. To wait, and hope that she would hook a good catch.

If she had felt like wavering in her decision to open Hell, one thing would have strengthened her determination, and that was the behaviour of the Embercombes. It occurred to her that they might well wonder how she was managing to live, and ought to feel in duty bound to assist her, since they knew nothing of Harry's gift and were aware that Sophia was penniless. But they did nothing. Perhaps it was another way of trying to drive her into Carbern's arms? And still she had no word from Harry. For all she knew, letters had arrived, and Lady Cecily had kept them from her.

In fact, Harry was on the point of sailing from the West Indies, barely recovered from a bad bout of fever. There was no point in writing letters; he would arrive as soon as the mail.

His thoughts of reunion with Kate were not entirely unclouded. All was not well at home, he was sure of that. Her letters, while still breathing affection for him, were uncommunicative and short; while his mother's gave the impression that although she did not wish to trouble him, something was amiss. He read between the lines. Kate was out much in society; Kate shared some of the pleasures of the fast set, but the Countess could not think there was any real harm in it; Kate saw very little of Edward, and left his care to the nursemaids, but that was not unusual, and his grandmother kept a close watch on his upbringing. Harry was too concerned with the allusions to Kate to recall that the same Lady Cecily had virtually ignored his existence until he was ten, and had allowed him to become a midshipman at fourteen.

So what did it mean? Kate was enjoying a round of

social pleasures. Was that so surprising, when she was deprived of her husband's company? But it was risky: he had warned her against that, and yet she had friends in the fast set, there was no knowing where that might lead. Or rather, one knew only too well, if a woman became involved with the rakes and the bloods. But not Kate —surely not Kate? And she had had such plans about caring for the baby, yet now she was no better than the average mother in high society. She was young to have the responsibility of a child; yet plenty of women had children when as young or younger. She knew Edward was not being neglected. All the same, he was not able to reassure himself, and knew he would not be easy until he was back home.

The date given by Kate had arrived; evening came. She dressed with care. Then she covered her face, head and shoulders with a hood, and went up the dark garden into the Gay Street house.

The cook and the kitchen boy were already busy; Hobley's men were arriving, and under his supervision they began to set up the tables in the gaming-room. Time ticked on; would the gamblers come? What a dreadful fiasco it would be if, in spite of her careful letter, they decided it was a trap to rob them and kept away. Suppose only one or two men came? That would be nearly as bad; there would be no atmosphere, nothing to make them return another night with more men. She had spent a lot of money on setting up the venture; she was gambling, if anyone was. Suppose she lost it all? Now there was nothing more she could do, she had tried to ensure success in every possible way. She must wait.

It was past the time given in her letter, and no one had come.

'Don't worry, madam,' said Hobley. (He had been instructed to give her nothing but this title.) 'Such men are never punctual.'

They waited.

There were noises outside the house. The knocker sounded. Kate hurried upstairs; Hobley went to the door.

Seven or eight men entered.

'Leave the door, man,' said one. 'There are more behind us.'

The fish had risen to the bait.

There were the Lords Carbern and Cambrell; a brace of baronets—Sir Claude Vernett and Sir Augustus Dee, close cronies of Carbern; two Honourables, each the son of a Viscount; Earl Markyate, bosom friend of Cambrell, and quite as dissolute; and several young men, sprigs of the nobility, already known for their addiction to high play.

They looked round the hall. Nicely furnished, well lit with candles in wall-sconces, it looked like the hall of a superior private house, and there was nothing to indicate the place was intended for any unusual purpose.

'Damme if I know what to make of this establishment,' said Carbern.

'Faith, we were led to believe we would find some amusement here!' bleated Sir Claude.

'What is going on, my man?' demanded Cambrell of the servant who had admitted them—Hobley himself.

'You know, sire, that you have been invited to join a gentlemen's club. The owner is relying on your discretion, for if the club is talked about it may well have unwelcome attention from the law. So we do not advertise ourselves at the front door. Now, if you will follow me, gentlemen, you will learn more.'

First he led them into a room off the hall where he requested their letters of invitation and checked their names against a list. Then he gave them some preliminary explanations.

'What is your name, man?' demanded Earl Markyate. 'Are you the owner here?'

'Here, sir, we are all anonymous,' was the reply. 'You will meet the owner upstairs.'

With this, he preceded them up to the next floor, and showed them into an anteroom. This was somewhat dark, for it was furnished in shades of grey, and opposite the entrance was a large double door painted black picked out with gold.

'A sombre-looking place,' said Carbern, 'and our cicerone does not look a very cheerful fellow.'

It was true; he was an enigmatic figure, lean, dark-skinned, with a face that showed no emotion but had the look of a man who could take care of himself. While the gentlemen were all finely dressed in brocades and silks richly coloured and embroidered, he stood out in complete contrast, clad in a black coat and knee breeches, the only colour being the sharp contrast of a scarlet waistcoat.

Now he moved over to the black double door and knocked twice. It was opened wide, and a woman stood there. They saw the outline of a slim figure against the brightness of the candles behind her; she moved forward, and several of the men gasped.

She was clad in a gown of black, with red flounces, but what had shocked them was the fact that her head and shoulders were completely covered by a black hood like an executioner's, through the slits of which her eyes gleamed and a red mouth partly showed. They could see nothing that would give them a clue as to her age, her

looks, her identity. All the womanly tell-tales—colour
of hair, texture of skin, firmness of rounded arms—all
were hidden. She stood for a long moment, her head
moving slightly as her gaze went from one to another, as
if checking on them. Then she spoke, in a voice low-
pitched, clear and strong.

'Good evening, gentlemen. Welcome to Hell! I am
Madam Satan.'

She turned, and motioned them to the inside room.
There they could now see a line of men, all dressed as the
first in black with scarlet waistcoats, each man masked.

'Here are my devils,' she went on. 'They are ready to
serve you. Whenever you choose, gentlemen, play may
begin.'

Borne on a wave of curiosity, the men trooped inside.
Here there were so many candles, that coming from the
dark anteroom they were momentarily dazzled. They
saw a room set out with tables and chairs, cards and dice,
everything ready for play. Here the walls were dark red,
and the long curtains over the windows were of a change-
able taffetta in bright red and orange, which the shifting
candlelight turned into sheets of flame.

A wolfish smile came to Carbern's lips. 'So this is
Hell!' he said slowly. 'A pretty conceit! And with the
cards and the dice, I own I feel quite at home here.'

He turned to the hooded woman.

'And what other delights are you providing for us,
Madam Satan?'

She answered in one long, low syllable.

'None.

Then she added, 'If your time at the tables should
make you hungry or thirsty, sir, my kitchen and cellar
will provide simple wholesome food and reasonable
wine.'

'Gad, no women!' exclaimed Sir Augustus.

She turned to him, the eyes in the dark hood glittering. 'This is a gambling club, sir—not a brothel. If you want whores, Bath is full of them, but you must go elsewhere.'

'Well said, Madam Satan!' Carbern exclaimed. 'Don't be such a fool, Gussie! Women don't mix with serious play—such distractions can come afterwards. This seems to me a promising establishment—but if you prefer that sleazy rat-hole we were in the other night, then, devil take you—go there!'

'Gad, Carbern, don't take me up so! I'm happy to stay here.'

By now the masked 'devils' had moved to their positions.

'The pleasures of Hell await you, gentlemen,' said Madam Satan. 'You may play any game you wish—provided that those which need them have my devils for bankers.'

Without more delay the men chose their games, their partners and opponents, and settled down to the serious business of the evening.

The night wore on; the air grew thick with tobacco smoke; the players at intervals felt the pangs of hunger or thirst, and were served from the kitchen with wine, with pies and cold meats; those too absorbed in play to wish for a pause could have the bread-and-meat snacks newly invented by that great gambler the Earl of Sandwich. No attempt was made to press the men to play against the bank; to be able to play among themselves would give them confidence in the house, Kate thought; they would come round to the other games later, and meanwhile she would have the subscription money and something from the sale of food and wine. For a time she must be satisfied to break even; profits would come later.

Kate took no part in the play, but moved about the room from table to table, checking on the efficiency of her devils, noting the preferences and play of the various gamblers. In the thickening atmosphere and with the excitement of gaming, the men were growing flushed and dishevelled; cravats had been cast off, wigs pushed back or discarded, coats and waistcoats unbuttoned or flung aside. She herself was feeling the discomfort of the heat and the close atmosphere, but was determined to stay as long as there were players, and to keep a clear head. She refreshed herself occasionally with sips of cold white wine, nothing more.

She passed, glass in hand, by the table where Carbern sat. He was no longer the immaculate sophisticate, but looked the rake he was. Coat and waistcoat gone, he sat in his shirtsleeves, his cropped head bare, his face somewhat flushed with wine and gambling fever. His teeth showed in that wolfish smile as his hand reached out and grasped her wrist.

Kate stood stock still.

'Let me go, sir,' she said coldly. 'Keep your hands for the cards.'

She sensed that Hobley had come up behind her.

'Why so? I find you devilish attractive, Madam Satan.'

She knew he was a man who delighted in power; among his associates he was the bear-leader, he enjoyed making women submit to him, now he intended to dominate her. This was going to be a battle of wills and she would not give. He must know that if he tried to rule her his friends would lose their amusement.

She would not give him the pleasure of physically struggling with him, but stood and looked down at him steadily, thankful he could not see the blood draining from her face as she fought the nausea the violent repulsion she felt for him engendered. Then she spoke calmly, in the deeper voice she had assumed to disguise her natural tones.

'In Hell, sir, you must abide by my rules, or leave. One person who breaks the rules may spoil the enjoyment of everyone. Let it be understood that I do not choose to be any man's plaything. Pray do not hold up your game.'

For a long moment he looked up at her, still smiling, his fingers tight upon her wrist. She held her glass in her other hand, and stilled the impulse to throw its contents in his face; Hobley stood behind her, poised, ready to act if she wished. Carbern took her measure; he could not see her pallor, only the unblinking gaze she levelled at him. No one moved.

Then he gave a light laugh and let her go.

'As you wish, Madam Satan.'

He turned to the man on his left. 'I always said the Devil was a fortunate fellow. Still, I find Hell so enjoyable, I'll not poach on his preserves.'

With a perfectly steady hand Kate raised her glass to her lips; then she motioned Hobley back to his place and moved unhurriedly to the next table.

The first night had been a success, there was no doubt of that. When the last gamblers left, Kate saw the cards and dice packed away and locked up in a concealed cupboard and her devils off the premises before she and Hobley made their way back to the house in Miles's Buildings. A good start, she thought. Now I must build on that foundation.

Hell had to operate in secret; everyone who came had

to be selected by Kate or vouched for by a member, and under such conditions it was surprising how quickly it prospered. She had a flair for organisation, and she positively enjoyed her new enterprise. Every evening she was on the look-out for details which could be improved, and as she moved among the tables she was learning all the time. Before too long, she promised herself, I shall surprise them. I shall take a table and be a banker. But for the time being she would stand back and content herself with seeing that everything went smoothly.

Soon Hell was full each night. The closed society of the bloods enjoyed so secret a business—they kept its existence to themselves, and gossiped about it in private. Each man had his own theory. One decided that Madam Satan was so hideously marked by smallpox that she could not show her face and mix in public, and this was her diversion; another believed her to be the discarded mistress of a person so high ranking—and so mean —that she had been obliged to choose this incognito method of making a living; another that she had been set up in business by the mayor of Bath and his cronies, to make money for them in a way they were officially committed to suppress. Each day someone propounded a new and more fantastic explanation. Only Carbern had no theory; he sat and listened, smiling that rapacious smile.

He did not lay hands on Kate again, but in the intervals of play his eyes followed her everywhere, as if in time his gaze would penetrate the hood and reveal her identity to him. There was no doubt he was piqued to find a woman in charge of Hell. She felt it was time she made her authority quite plain.

The club was well established and thriving when Kate

decided to give this evidence. Gaming had gone on for some hours one evening when she went over to the faro table at which one of her devils was banker to five players.

'Devil Three, I shall take the bank,' she said.

The players looked up in surprise as the dealer gave her his seat. She took the cards and shuffled. Tonight she was wearing sleeves that finished at the elbow; her slim arms and well-shaped hands were in full view as she shuffled. Her handling of the cards was as expert as any man's, and she saw the critical gaze of the players turn to grudging approval.

She set up the cards. Play recommenced. She knew the men were waiting for her to make a mistake, but she was not going to give them that satisfaction. She turned the cards, she managed the bets for over an hour, she ran the faro table and there could be no complaints. Then —the bank considerably enriched, she was glad to note —she gave the chair back to a devil and moved on, satisfied that she had shown the men she knew her business.

She was totally unaware that while she sat at the faro table, Harry Breedon was on a ship nearing the coast of Britain, longing for a sight of Portsmouth and the English shore, yearning for his wife and baby son.

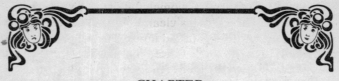

CHAPTER
EIGHT

CARBERN WAS piqued. More than that, he felt himself challenged. He had never met a woman who assumed and carried off a position of authority in a sphere where men ruled, and he found it most provoking. In addition his curiosity was roused more strongly every night by the fact that this woman never showed her face.

Was she so hideous that she would not allow herself to be seen—or did she scorn to rule men by reason of her beauty, as women were expected to do? She was young, and moved with grace, her hands and arms were soft and supple, she was slim, but had the curves which promised all the pleasure a man could expect a woman to provide, and, quite possibly, delights above such expectations.

Who could she be? Carbern was baffled. He knew the society of Bath, but such women must be ruled out. He knew the *demi-mode* equally well, but could not think of anyone who matched up to Madam Satan; and as for the low classes, the madams of the brothels and the girls of the whore-houses, the 'laced mutton' with which he was not unacquainted—such women could not possibly possess the style, the speech, the manner that came naturally to this mysterious young person.

It was intriguing, too, that she concentrated exclusively on gaming. She had made it plain from the beginning that if they wanted women they must go elsewhere. In every way, Hell was a clean house. He had kept his eyes open, and had satisfied himself that there were no marked cards, no loaded dice, and that the devils could not be faulted at the deal. And so everything provoked him into greater speculation over the identity of Madam Satan.

Carbern was not a man who let himself remain unsatisfied in any particular. He decided it was worth while putting himself to some inconvenience to gratify his curiosity. This was not a matter he could hire a man to do for him, and to be rewarding it must be kept secret. So, one night, when the gaming was over and he and his cronies left Hell, he refused all invitations to finish off the night elsewhere and pretended to return to his apartments. Instead, as soon as he was alone, he doubled back and took up a position to watch the house in Gay Street.

It was still dark, and there was very little moon, but before long he saw the gleam of a lantern below the area steps and figures coming up and passing through the gate into the street. He tried to count them—they were the devils, he was sure that no female figure was among them. He did not expect there would be; Madam Satan no doubt lived on the premises. The sombre figures moved on, and he thought he had heard a door being shut and bolted; he now gave his attention to the windows.

All the gamblers had seen of the house was the hall and one room beside it, the stair case, the anteroom and the gaming-room on the first floor. The kitchen quarters would be in the basement; there must be two rooms on the ground floor and one more on the first floor, with the whole second floor and the attic rooms above which they had not seen; enough space for private rooms for the proprietress and a servant or two.

Now, if Madam was going to bed, surely some lights would show? Somewhere there would be a chink between the curtains, or someone would come to a window; there would be the gleam of candles. He waited. Nothing. The house front stayed blind and black. What could be going on? Was it possible that she was in the basement with the living-in servants? He discounted that at once. Possibly she was still in the gaming-room, checking on the night's takings; she might wait until the devils had left to do that. He visualised her, in the room with most of the candles extinguished, sitting at a table with a branch-light beside her, taking the gold coins in her slim fingers, counting and piling them up. Her face—her hair—what were they like? She would have taken off her hood by now. She must be young—but how young? Would her looks be well favoured enough to increase the attraction she had for him, or was she so ugly that he would find her instantly repulsive?

Damnation! Something should be happening by now. He was getting cold and stiff, lurking about against a house railing after the heat of the gaming-room. He was also running the risk of being set upon and robbed by any passing group of ruffians who took it into their heads to risk the fashionable part of town. Luckily so far the street had remained deserted. Perhaps she was having supper served now—she never touched food in their presence. Hell's teeth, how much longer would he be fool enough to wait? What was he waiting for? Then he cursed himself under his breath, long, fluently, exhaustively, for the idiot he was. There was a possibility he had totally overlooked.

Suppose she did not spend the night in the house

—what then? If she slept somewhere else, she would not go on foot. But no carriage had arrived and no chair had come to the house while he had been there; was it possible she had left before the devils? Possible, yes; but, he thought, unlikely. Then what other explanation could there be? He tried to picture her within the house—and in a flash it came to him.

At the back of these houses there were gardens. Would there not be access to them from the basements? And from the garden there might well be a way out to a mews or an alley. Madam Satan was quite unconventional enough to make use of that. In fact, it would be to her advantage. She could leave the house hooded; but by the time she had made her way to where she would have a carriage or a chair waiting for her, she would have taken off that all-concealing hood and become, instead of the mistress of a gaming-house, an upper-class woman returning from an assignation.

Swiftly he walked along the lower part of Gay Street, turning down George Street where it intersected, and looking left, cast an eye at what could be seen of the rear of the upper part of Gay Street. He was right; there were gardens at the back. The ends were shut off by a high wall, so he could not see the back doors, but each house had a door in the end wall giving from the garden on to a narrow street, with more houses on the opposite side. He counted the garden doors; having settled from that which was the house he should watch, he was gratified to see it was the only one from which a glimmer of light showed. Then, upstairs, the light went out.

The garden wall prevented him from seeing whether the basement showed the faint gleam of candles. It was very quiet all about, for the town had gone to sleep at last. He jumped as a dog started barking. He listened carefully, for he did not want to be savaged by a loose watch-dog, but the dog was not free, he could hear the chain rattling as it moved; he set to wondering whether he could improve his vantage-point. But he decided to stay where he was; if the way was not a cul-de-sac, the exit was certainly very narrow, and he had no wish to be trapped or even observed there. Not that there was much risk of being recognised, for there was little moon, and that fitfully obscured by scudding cloud. No, he was safer here, where he could slip away as soon as someone came in his direction.

He would have felt happier if he had heard the sound of carriage wheels or the grumbling exchanges of a couple of chairmen in George Street, waiting for a regular customer. But the night was utterly still, and he was on the point of giving up and leaving when he heard the sound of a door opening. More sounds; the door was being shut and locked; still he waited, and now he was sure. Someone was coming down a garden path—was it the right one? Then a bolt creaked, and the door he was watching began to open.

He could see a faint light showing round the edge as it swung wide, as if someone was carrying a lantern. Now the restricted beam was directed on to the path, showing the way for someone to tread; and straining his eyes, Carbern thought he saw two figures. The metallic sound of the door-latch had carried on the still air; but at a distance the figures seemed to be moving noiselessly, passing like shadows. The lantern threw a glow about their feet, and with a sudden rush of excitement he thought he glimpsed the bulk of a woman's long full skirts. The two figures did not move as he had expected, either up or down the street. They crossed it, and went direct to the front door opposite them. A moment more, and they had both slipped into the house in Miles's Buildings.

Harry guessed that his return would be totally unexpected. During the long voyage he had had plenty of time to think of the future. He realised that through his absence from home he had been sustained, not by a boy's infatuation for Annabel Harcourt, but by a man's deep affection for his irritating, intelligent and most delightful wife, and by the thought of the son she had borne him. Life at sea had lost its compulsive attraction for him; he was disillusioned by the fact he could do so little for the men who were supposed to be in his care, and he had decided to resign his commission.

What he would do on land he did not yet know; that was something he would discuss with Kate, she was never short of ideas; and whatever was wrong at home would be cleared up by his return. He landed at Portsmouth and set off by stage to Bath, knowing that it was the time of year when the family would be at Queen Square.

Kate was well satisfied with her venture. Hell was prospering; the money in her bank deposit, at first greatly depleted by the expenses of setting up the club, was recovered and increased. The staff were working well, and seemed trustworthy. Hobley had made a good job of selecting the 'devils'. Over and above this, Kate was finding a perverse satisfaction in her role of gaming-house keeper. For once in her life she was getting the better of men; she had turned their greed and dissipation to her own account.

Besides, without the club, what would she do? Sitting at home, she could only brood on the loss of husband

and child. She could not decide whether she had been right or wrong to leave Edward to the Embercombes, but she knew she could not have endured the alternative. She could bear the sorrow of parting better than the total humiliation to which she would have been subjected. To have but half an hour a day with her child —and that subject to the caprice of Lady Cecily—to know that he was being brought up in a way she did not approve, to be another spoilt, selfish, arrogant Embercombe; to guess that his mind was being poisoned against her into the bargain; to see him as a privilege, as if she were there on sufferance; it would have soured and twisted her and probably have sent her half-crazy. No, she would employ herself by running Hell, and wait for Harry's return.

She did not let herself look far into the future. She would not want to keep Hell running indefinitely, but at present it was serving her purpose; it gave her a bitter satisfaction, it brought her profit, and it kept her from brooding.

Kate was not an early riser now that she stayed at the club till the small hours of the morning, and she had not been long downstairs when the maid announced a caller. It was Lord Carbern. She would not have expected him to be up and about; more surprising that he should call, for he had no reason to know where she lived, and keeping out of society as she did she had encountered him only once since leaving Queen Square. She did not wish to see him now, and sent a message that she was not receiving.

The maid returned, looking awkward and confused.

'M'lady, the gentleman says he must see you, and will wait downstairs until you are ready. He has something of importance to discuss.'

She had better see him, Kate thought; she must tell the servants that if he came again he was not to be admitted.

Carbern's valet had done a good job, he was transformed from last night's rake into an elegant dandy. Last night he had been sweating in his shirtsleeves, throat and cropped head bare, face flushed and eyes bloodshot. Now he was sartorial perfection in a plum-coloured brocade coat, buff corded silk breeches, lace ruffles and impeccable wig. He gave Kate an elaborate bow and an affable greeting.

Kate, who was wishing that Sophia would appear, responded.

'Good morning, Lord Carbern. I am surprised that you know where I live, and I cannot imagine what brings you here.'

'Oh, one can always find out where beauty resides, and you should know that your charms are enough to attract me from any distance.'

'Well, the distance was not far. But I must ask you to resist the impulse in future, for I have nothing to say to you.'

His eyes swept over her and he lapsed into familiarity.

'Come, Kate, you are not giving me a dismissal, I hope? For I have a few important words to say to you.'

'I cannot think what they could be,' she answered coldly.

'Can you not? It has occurred to me that now you are no longer living at Queen Square in the Embercombe household you may look more kindly on my proposal. You're a deuced attractive woman, Kate, and worthy of a better establishment than this wretched little house.'

'This wretched little house is my choice. And just what is your proposal, Lord Carbern?'

He went through an elaborate business of snuff-taking before replying, which he eventually did with a cool insolence that made Kate's heart race with anger.

'My dear, I am prepared to set you up in style and comfort. You shan't want for clothes and trinkets, either. In return, of course, I shall have full—and exclusive—enjoyment of your charms, which will be ample repayment.'

'I see. I was right—I have nothing to say to you. Please leave.'

'You can't get rid of me as quickly as that, Kate. It's devilish uncomplimentary not to give my offer a little more consideration.'

He lounged back and would not take his eyes off her, and there was a smile on his lips and a confidence in his manner that she found disquieting.

'There is nothing to consider.'

He laughed. 'Do not think you can fence with me. Oh, I like a woman who doesn't give in easily! But you'll surrender, and it will give me the greatest pleasure to bed you.'

Kate would have risen to leave the room, but at her first move he anticipated her, and his hand shot out and seized her wrist. His indolence, his casual manner, had gone in a flash. His other arm came across, and now she was trapped in the corner of the sofa, his glittering eyes challenging her, his teeth bared in a hard, gloating smile.

'You may as well come to terms with me, for I decided to have you long ago. I have been patient, but I'll not wait much longer. Now I have a card up my sleeve which will force your hand, and if needs be, I'll use it.'

He laughed again as she struggled futilely, and then

went on, 'You'll be glad to come to me, rather than be hauled into the magistrate's court and thrown out of society. What a juicy bit of gossip—what a nine days' wonder—when Bath discovers that the prudish little Viscountess who will be neither wife nor mistress is none other than Madam Satan!'

She could not control the flick of her eyelids, the jerk of shock, but she pulled herself together and retorted, 'Let me go! I don't know what you're talking about.'

'It's no good. That look of yours gave you away. Now we know where we stand.'

His hand went up to caress her neck, then his fingers clasped themselves, lightly at first, around her throat.

'Just think about it, little Kate. If I open my mouth, your denials won't serve you for long. You—the known madam of a gaming-house! Being my mistress will be a sight more comfortable.'

His fingers tightened.

'I'll not let you go this time. Damme, I find you a deuced sight more attractive now I know what you do in your spare time. We'll make a fine pair, you and I! We'll keep Hell going, it will be amusing. No one will know that Madam Satan has a mate at last—that I am your Lucifer.'

He dragged her closer and set his mouth on hers in a kiss of cruel and sensuous intimacy. His hand left her throat and passed possessively over her body. She was revolted by his touch, sickened by the smell of sweat and perfume, tobacco smoke and drink which clung to his skin and his clothes. Panic began to rise within her. At last he let her fight free.

'Gad, I feel drunk at the thought of making you my pretty little whore! But I'll give you a couple of days to consider my offer. Time to bring you to your senses and

sharpen my appetite even more. You've no choice, my
dear. You had better hope that if you please me enough I
may even abandon my principles and consider marrying
you when Stonebridge legally rids himself of you. Give
my desires superlative satisfaction, and you might earn
that reward in time. It's worth thinking about!'

He gave her one long, gloating, triumphant look, and
left. Kate sat there, sick and trembling, feeling that she
had been stripped naked.

Harry Breedon arrived at Queen Square and marched
into the house, expecting at every moment to hear
Kate's light step and welcoming voice, to see her face
light up with amazed pleasure as she met him. But she
did not come; his first encounter was with his mother.

'Harry! What a surprise! Why, how thin and tired you
look!'

'Mama! It is splendid to be home! Where is Kate?'

His mother replied with some constraint, 'She is not
here.'

'Evidently! But where is she? Gone to the park with
Edward and the nurse?'

'No. You will want to see Edward now. He is a fine
boy.'

'Mama, where *is* Kate?' Her evasion struck him with a
sudden fear. 'She is not dead?'

'*Dead?* Oh no, whatever made you think of that?
Ah—here is your father.'

The men greeted each other warmly.

'Now, tell me,' Harry went on. '*Where is Kate?*'

His mother shrugged. 'Well, you must know sooner or
later. She has left us.'

'Left you? For how long? Where—?'

Lady Cecily answered with no hesitation, 'It is no

more than we might have expected. She simply packed up her things and left.'

'*And you let her?*'

'I could not stop her. I can find no excuse for her behaviour. It was most extraordinary. She abandoned Edward to our care, and went to live with Sophia Spenlow.'

Harry's face grew pale. 'In God's name, why? Did you not ask?'

'I suppose she found life dull here. She was not blessed with maternal instincts, and she spent little time with the babe. With Sophia, she can live as she chooses. That girl is so weak that if Kate took another man, she would turn a blind eye.'

'*If Kate*—are you suggesting . . .!'

'It would not surprise me. She is a healthy young woman, and there are plenty of men here who find her attractive.'

He could not believe it of Kate. But something was very wrong.

'You have kept in touch with her?'

'Why should I, after the manner of her leaving? If she could abandon Edward . . .'

'But for all you know she might be penniless! We are all aware that Sophia has no money of her own, and young Spenlow gambles . . .'

'She seems well provided for, from whatever source.'

'From whatever source! And that is all you can say! You let her go, and did nothing! In God's name, *Kate is my wife*!'

With that he turned and strode out of the room, too concerned to notice that his father had not said a single word.

Harry's mind was in a turmoil. His mother's remarks

kept ringing in his brain: '. . . not blessed with maternal instincts . . .', yet her letters had been full of affection for Edward. '. . . if Kate took another man . . . it would not surprise me . . .' Kate, who had written with such love to him—had it all been a pretence? He could not believe it, that was not Kate, and yet a fact was a fact—she was not living at Queen Square. One quick enquiry had given him her address, so, confused and anxious, he made his way to Miles's Buildings.

Harry's arrival caught Kate when she was still off balance. Carbern had left her with two appalling alternatives—to be his mistress, which she could not and would not consider—or to face exposure. She had no illusions that to defy him might cause him to show any mercy. Of course, she could deny she was Madam Satan, and he could not prove the assertion except by unmasking her in the club, which with her 'devils' she could prevent, but the proximity of the Miles's Buildings house to the back of Gay Street would be seen to be no coincidence. There were enough pointers for Bath society to accept his word against hers, and everyone would delight in such a sensational scandal. Life for her in Bath would soon be unbearable. Her mind was still filling in the grim details of the picture when the door of the drawing-room opened, and she turned to see Harry on the threshold.

The shock was so great that her legs almost gave way as she jumped to her feet, and she practically fell into his arms.

'*Harry!* Oh, Harry, my dearest!'

He held her close, burying his face in her hair, stroking and kissing it while broken phrases came from his lips.

'Kate—sweet Kate—God, how I've missed you! I've longed for this moment—but why are you here?'

'You've been to Queen Square—you've seen Edward?'

'No—I came to find you.'

'*You haven't seen him!* Your own son!'

He took her by the shoulders and held her so that he could gaze into her eyes.

'And you have left him—your own son! Why?'

Her look of love changed into one of defiance.

'Did they not tell you? No, of course they wouldn't. No one would say that Lady Cecily made my life unbearable, ruled the nursery and finally would only allow me to see Edward for half an hour each day . . .'

'Kate, what are you saying?' His look was incredulous. 'She could not do that! What reason could she possibly have?'

'You don't believe me? What tales has she told you?'

'She said very little—only that you must have found life dull, and that with Sophia you could live as you choose . . .'

He could not bring himself to say more.

'And you think I would *choose* to live without Edward? You think it was an easy decision for me? Harry, it nearly broke my heart—but believe me, I could not stay in that house on your mother's conditions, it would have driven me melancholy mad!'

He was silent for a moment, looking down at her. He wanted to believe her, and yet the two versions were irreconcilable. It would take time to get at the truth of it, and he was not sure he wanted to.

'My dear, I'm home now, and home to stay. You and my mother have had your differences, that is plain, but now we can forget all that. Come back with me, make friends, and start again.'

'Make friends! With your mother! She hates me . . .'

'Oh, Kate, don't start making difficulties the moment I'm back!'

'I'm sorry, Harry. Oh, my dear, this is so wonderful . . .'

'Then come home, and introduce me to our son.'

She gave a short laugh. '*I* shall have to be introduced to him.'

'Never mind. Everything will soon settle down. Come along.'

Kate could see it all. The return to Queen Square, and being treated like one fallen from grace who has to be accepted; hearing the subtle remarks laced with poison for Harry's benefit; of the nursery tyranny being cunningly contrived to keep her out of Edward's affections —and she rebelled.

'I can't, Harry. Not now, not like that. I can't live under the same roof as your parents. Please, Harry, get a house, bring Edward and let the three of us live together.'

He looked shocked.

'Kate, what an extraordinary suggestion! I have just returned, and you want me to leave my parents' house and set up separately? Even though you have had your differences, it is . . .'

'*Differences*! You don't know! Oh, *we* are a family, Harry. We should live together.'

'And so we can, at Queen Square.'

'No! I won't go back there to live with your mother.'

'How can you be so unreasonable the moment I return!'

'Unreasonable! You have no idea what my life has been like . . .'

'Mine has not been a flower-strewn path! Well, then, tell me!'

His look was not sympathetic—how could she expect it to be? In her mind Kate made a lightning survey of the time since he left and saw a catalogue of woe which would only arouse impatience and disbelief if she began to tell him now. He would see it as a succession of complaints against his mother—and to him, most of them would be incredible. It would sour their relationship.

'No, not now, Harry. I don't want to spoil your homecoming.'

'I'm glad of that! So you'll call a truce, and come.'

'Not today, Harry. I can't leave Sophia without warning.'

'*Sophia*, now! Gad, I'm your husband, Kate! Don't you realise—I have come home—I want a wife!'

'It cannot hurt to wait a few days . . . to be together. You can soon rent a house . . .'

His arms dropped away from her. 'You're making excuses! *Why?*'

'I can't explain now. Give me a day or two—bring Edward to a place where we can all be together.'

'I thought you'd be glad to see me, but now you hold me off—*why*? Is there someone else?'

'*No!*' She was shocked and angry at the suggestion. 'Harry, why can't we just be happy together? Don't spoil this moment . . .'

'I think it is already spoilt. I can't stand these evasions.'

'Nor will you like anything I can say about my life since you left. If you want unbiased information, I suggest you go to Mr Dewley the lawyer, and ask why I consulted him.'

'You consulted a *lawyer*? Why? About the legality of our marriage?'

'*No!* You must ask him. You would find it hard to believe me.'

'Would I? Then why should I believe him? Still, I'll go.'

'Harry—not this instant! We've only had a few minutes . . .'

'And been at loggerheads for most of them! This must be cleared up. I'll come back later. I hope you will receive me as a husband, and not as an inconvenient caller!'

Kate was stunned. It was all too much. A few minutes of joy, of ecstasy at being in Harry's arms again, and then the new happiness was shattered. Was it all her fault? Should she have gone back and endured whatever treatment Lady Cecily might have in store for her? To be reunited with Harry and Edward, she should have been prepared to stand anything. But couldn't Harry have been a little more understanding, a little less inflexible?

Then in the back of her mind was another thought —what would she do about Hell? The club must be wound up, that was plain. Harry's return made it imperative. Would he ever forgive her if he found out what she had been doing? But she could not shut Hell without warning. She must stay a few nights more in Miles's Buildings to arrange for its closure. She told herself that Harry's return made it unlikely that Carbern would carry out his threat, but she could not feel easy about that. What should she do?

Harry left Miles's Building in worse case than he arrived. He did not want to believe his mother's insinuations, and yet without that possibility nothing seemed to make sense. Why should Kate not come back with him? He thought she had been overjoyed to see him—yet the delight had not lasted. She would not—or could not

—give one good reason for her refusal to return to Queen Square. And she was his wife! If he got a carriage and took her back by force, he would be within his rights. But that wouldn't do for Kate. Some women might like it—not Kate.

She had referred him to a lawyer. He could not imagine why she could have needed to consult one. He had better find out, be the reason good or ill. It was not difficult to get Mr Dewley's address, but to his chagrin when he arrived at the office he was told that the lawyer was away on business, and it was not a matter Harry cared to discuss with a clerk. So he left unsatisfied. He supposed he must have another talk with his parents and try to get matters clearer.

He couldn't face that now. Hunger and worry were combining to turn his stomach, and whether he fancied it or not, he needed food. But not at Queen Square. He looked about him. He was now in the centre of town. There must be an inn or a chop-house near by, and he soon found a respectable-looking place, and went inside.

Taking a table in a corner of the comfortable dining-room, he settled himself with a mug of ale. He did not want company, and he was too deep in his thoughts to notice whether any of the other men in the room were known to him.

Richard Stukely, just finishing his meal, looked up from the snug corner where he sat to see a tall man, lean and dark, whose face was vaguely familiar, come in and seat himself at the other side of the room. He looked at him idly, then with a sudden shock he recognised Harry Breedon. Resentment still burned within him for the horsewhipping Breedon had given him. He had never ceased to harbour a strong desire to pay him back in some kind. And there was one delightful way in which scores could now be evened—nothing as crude as a beating in return for the horsewhipping, but something from which Breedon would never escape, like a thorn in the flesh leaving a suppurating wound which would never heal.

Stukely finished his meal at leisure, turning over the plan—derived from an idea which had occurred to him long since—in his mind, savouring in advance the pleasure he would have in delivering his blow. He had an extra brandy on the strength of it, and then, not by any means drunk, but fortified against whatever reaction should come from Breedon, he got to his feet and strolled across the room.

'Gad, if it isn't Stonebridge returned at last!' he exclaimed.

Harry looked up and saw Stukely. His hatred of the man immediately flashed to the surface. He had every reason not to be civil. He made no acknowledgement.

To his surprise, Stukely pulled out a chair opposite him and sat down.

'Had a rough time overseas, did you?' Stukely went on. 'And now you have returned to the bosom of your rejoicing family, no doubt.'

Does he know, Harry wondered, that my wife has left the family home?

'I trust you found everyone well?' said Stukely smoothly.

The piggy eyes in the broad red face were appraising him, the loose mouth smiling slightly. I wish to God he'd go, Harry thought; why is he inflicting himself on me? He must have the hide of a rhinoceros.

'Travel has not made you talkative, it seems. I expect you were delighted to find you have been blessed with a

son and heir in your absence. I hear he's a fine strong
boy.'

'He is.'

That at least was a safe reply.

Stukely smiled a little wider.

'A strange thing about that boy,' he said thoughtfully.
'Did you ever consider the little matter of his birth
date? I own I was interested enough to make a small
calculation. You'll never know, will you, whether
the Embercombe heir is your boy, or whether he's
Richard Stukely's son.'

Harry gazed at him, his brain totally emptied by the
shock. Then he thought, the man's a lunatic. How could
he say such a thing? But Stukely went on smiling, and
after a long, deathly pause, he went on talking.

'Of course she told you I didn't finish the job on her.
Quite a natural reaction on her part—she would think of
the consequences if she had a child by me, and protect
the infant and herself. How shaming it would be for her
to have to admit to you that the heir after you to the
Embercombe title was really Richard Stukely's bastard.'

A red mist swam before Harry's eyes. If he had been
capable of movement he would have risen and caught
Stukely by the throat, choking the words and the man
himself into oblivion. But he was paralysed, unable to
move, to speak, almost unable to think. Almost, but not
quite. He could understand what Stukely was saying
—that if his rape of Katharine had been complete, it was
possible that Edward was Stukely's child.

At last something came through the bile that was
bitter in his throat and mouth, and resolved itself into
words.

'You . . . fool . . . liar !'

'Oh no. It's perfectly true. I'm not saying that he *is*,

but simply that it's possible. The dates fit. *She* says I
didn't seed her, *I* say I did. You'll never know the truth,
will you?'

And still smiling he got up and sauntered away,
leaving Harry, his face pale and fixed like a death mask,
staring at nothing.

CHAPTER
NINE

AFTER THE encounter with Stukely, it took Harry some time to pull himself together. He did his best to make reason conquer emotion. Stukely hated him; why should he credit a tale he had never before found cause to suspect? Kate's reaction at the time had been one of shuddering relief that the act had not been completed, and her delight in her pregnancy seemed unclouded. But if she had later had any suspicion, it could account for her leaving the child to the Embercombes. Yet why later, if not at the time? No, that made no sense. But what a homecoming he was having, he thought; nothing but bitterness and suspicion.

By evening Harry felt he could not face much more of his parents' society that day: his father's sustained bonhomie and his mother's interest in life in the West Indies both seemed to avoid any mention of Kate. He made an excuse to leave the house and went to the Assembly Rooms, hoping to find some congenial and undemanding old acquaintance. He was unlucky; only frivolous society was there. He drank a bottle of wine and played a few hands of whist in the card-room. He was then accosted by none other than Lord Carbern, who remarked that he looked 'demmed out of spirits and in need of distraction'.

'And I know the very place for you,' Carbern went on.

'It is new to you, and exclusive, but I can get you in. You'll find plenty to amuse you, I'll wager. The play isn't milk-and-water stuff, as it is here.'

Since he could not face his parents or Kate, he certainly needed distraction, as Carbern had said. With a feeling of slight relief but little enthusiasm, he agreed. A serious session at cards would demand all his concentration, and take his mind off his anxieties.

That evening Kate set out as usual for Gay Street. After such a nerve-jangling day it was something of an anticlimax that nothing in the club was different; the same faces, the same conversation; the grouping at the tables, the rattle of dice and the exclamations of the players; the flip-flap of cards and the calling of bids; and the heat, the smoke, the noise increasing as the night wore on.

Carbern was later than customary. For a while she hoped he might not be coming, but after play had been going on for some time he arrived. Coming up to her, he made a punctilious bow.

'Good evening, Madam Satan. I beg the favour of introducing a new member. He is, I assure you, most discreet; he is also quite gratifyingly solvent; and of a social position acceptable to everyone here. Will you take him on my recommendation?'

'I could hardly refuse, sir, since you speak of him in such glowing terms. When does he wish to join us?'

'Tonight, madam, for he is sorely in need of amusement. In fact, he is waiting now, outside. Shall I bring him in?'

'By all means.'

Carbern went to the door. A moment later he returned, and behind him was the shadow of a man as tall as he, and somewhat slimmer. The man came forward from the gloom of the ante room into the light of the saloon, and Kate found herself looking into the face of her husband.

Never before had Kate been so glad of her concealing hood. She suppressed the start of surprised recognition, willed her hands not to clench or flutter nervously, kept her breath shallow and even; but she knew that first she had gone pale, and then that the blood had returned to her cheeks and flooded them with a deep flush.

She must speak to him. Pray God he would not recognise the deeper tones of voice she had adopted!

'What is your preference, sir?'

'My preference?'

'What is your fancy, cards or dice?'

'Oh, cards,' he said easily. 'Dice are too random for me.'

'Cards, then, whatever game you choose. I will leave you in this gentleman's hands.'

She moved on. Hobley came up to her with a glass of wine. As she took it, he said, his face expressionless but his eyes shrewd,

'An odd turn-up of the cards, madam.'

'Yes,' she replied. 'My Lord Carbern has drawn the joker.'

Carbern had warned Harry about Madam Satan. 'The place is not an academy as well—she's no whore-mistress. She stands no nonsense from any man, and she covers her face and head with a hood so that no one may recognise her outside Hell.'

'Why should she be so fussy?'

Carbern took a pinch of snuff and answered languidly, 'No doubt she has her reasons, but we do not know them. No one, you see, has dared to ask.'

'Dared?'

'Egad, man, she rules us all. If we offend her, she will exclude us from Hell—and that is a punishment none wishes to endure. Hell is the only civilised place for a dedicated gambler.'

Harry was in no mood to be curious over the foibles of any woman, even if she should happen to be unique—he had never heard of a woman keeping a respectable gaming house before, though there were plenty of old bawds who provided card-play with their prostitutes as an additional method of fleecing their patrons. But a good gaming house was what he needed; the play might take his mind off Kate for a few hours. In his mind's eye he saw her, a little more mature than when he left, and still more beautiful. Annabel Harcourt—glimpsed a few minutes ago in the Assembly Rooms—could not hold a candle to her; she was already looking overblown, a rose whose pink and white petals were unnaturally painted. She was running to fat, but, worst of all, the sound of her inane lisping chatter made him think: Egad, what did I ever see in her? I must have been an idiot boy to find her attractive! But Kate—Kate was like a fine wine, she had improved with keeping. But to think of her now was too disturbing. An evening at the tables, concentrating on the cards—that would be the best medicine.

But as time passed, Harry's attention drifted from the cards to Madam Satan. To his surprise he found himself becoming fascinated by her. Here was a woman who was not an echo of any man, who accepted no domination, a woman who in an extraordinary sphere demonstrated positive abilities. Whether this was right and good was a moot point, but it made her exceptional. What lay under that hood? Was it a repellent ugliness, or a distracting beauty? Was it her whim to be masked, or a compelling need for anonymity? And there was something more

—he had the strange feeling that he might, at some time, have met her. Obviously she must belong to the *demimonde* to have chosen such an occupation; and he, who in sowing his wild oats had tasted most of the pleasures of such society, racked his brains, trying to recall the establishments he had visited and the ladies he had seen there. But he could think of no one who even remotely matched up to Madam Satan. It was frustrating, but no matter, it gave him something fresh to think about.

During the intervals of play, while he smoked and had desultory conversation, he covertly watched and listened. Rarely had he met a woman so informed, so well versed in the country's affairs; she must pick up her knowledge from the eminent people who frequented her tables, and she certainly made good use of it. Perhaps those members of Hell were right who said she knew so much because she was the ex-mistress of a politician or a man of letters? Ex-mistress—by God, thought Harry, I'd not have parted with her! He pondered that piece of gossip, and noted to himself that she did not wear the badges of a kept woman—she had no jewellery. That was unusual.

Madam Satan was now heading a faro table, and as she dealt the cards, Harry watched her slim, well-shaped hands, completely bare save for a plain narrow band on her wedding finger. Another thought came to his mind. He knew only one woman above the rank of servant or below the level of respectability who did not wear her fingers covered with rings. Kate—his own wife Kate! Except for rare social occasions when she was lent Embercombe jewellery, she wore nothing on her hands but the large knot ring he had given her on their marriage. Kate, and Madam Satan—it was an odd coincidence. That it was anything more than a coincidence was

quite impossible. Two women—two intelligent women
—both of whom disdained jewellery; but they were
poles apart, not only in circumstances and social standing but in experience and manner. Kate could never act
with such authority, such a confidence that at times came
close to an indifferent contempt towards some of the
men she was providing with entertainment. Or could
she? Were his wits going astray, that he could see any
similarity?

Hours passed and play grew more reckless, but Kate
noticed that Harry did not fall a victim to high stakes. He
went on playing piquet with a cool precision, apparently
oblivious to the noise and excitement around him. He
took some food, and drank sparingly. She wondered
why he had come—had Carbern lured him there for
some reason of his own? The dreadful thought struck her
that Carbern might press her for a decision that night, and
if she refused him, he might expose her on the spot. It
would be like him to inflict the maximum of pain on
anyone who crossed him.

She felt a sinking sensation in the pit of her stomach,
and when Carbern got up and lounged across to her, her
heart began to beat suffocatingly in her throat. He stood
with his back to the room, and spoke quietly so that no
one else could hear.

'Well, Madam Satan, have you come to a decision?'

'I understood I was to be given a day or two to think it
over,' she murmured, striving to show a calm she did not
feel.

'You cannot blame me for being impatient.'

'And you cannot blame me for weighing up the
alternatives.'

'Surely the matter has now become more urgent? A
certain gentleman has returned.'

'I had thought his arrival might put an end to your importunities.'

He gave a low, mocking laugh. 'On the contrary, it strengthens my hand. Disclosure, besides excluding you from society, would finish you with him and his family. Everyone knows you are already estranged from them, and have given up your son. Your husband would disown you as well. You really have no alternative now. Join forces with me willingly, and I shall keep my mouth shut. You will simply be an errant wife going off with another man. I am sure society would applaud you for leaving that cold fish and his boring parents for someone who will give you a spin on the merry-go-round and some lively companions.'

Desperately she thought: I must win time—time to close Hell, time to escape.

'Big decisions should not be hurried. You can afford to give me another day, since you are so sure of success. I need time to make some personal arrangements.'

'Don't tell me you wish to write farewell letters!' came the sneering whisper. 'Or perhaps kiss all the Embercombes goodbye?'

'That is my affair. Do I have another day?'

'Very well. Until this time tomorrow.' For a moment his hand gripped her wrist. 'Don't try to run away. You won't get far.'

She felt momentarily faint with fear as he left her. She took a glass of wine, and steadied herself to see the night out.

Harry did not sleep late after his session with the cards. He had decided to be up in good time in the hope of seeing Kate's lawyer, since she had almost made that a prerequisite to any further discussion. When, by mid-morning, he arrived at Mr Dewley's office, it was to find the lawyer in, and prepared to see him.

Mr Dewley was at first reluctant to discuss a client's affairs even with her husband, but what he eventually told Harry was enough to send him to see Harrington, the other lawyer concerned, whose name Mr Dewley gave him. He arrived at Mr Harrington's office in George Street looking troubled; he left with a brow black as thunder and made his way hot-foot back to Queen Square.

His parents were out, on a long-standing engagement, and did not return until late. Then the storm broke. The Embercombes saw a side of Harry they did not know existed: he was accusing, scathing, insistent; he refuted all their excuses and demolished all their arguments. He poured withering scorn on his father for being so weak and easily led into unpardonable actions; his mother he faced with cold fury. Finally she broke down; and he, having emptied the last dregs of his wrath on her, strode out of the house to seek out Kate in Miles's Buildings.

He saw, not Kate, but Sophia, who seemed quite disconcerted by his arrival, and he in turn was knocked off balance when she told him he could not see Kate.

'She is . . . already in bed. She is ill with a megrim, her head is aching so that she cannot speak to anyone.'

'Let me see her. I'll cure her megrim.'

'No, indeed, you must not see her, Harry. She is really far too sick. She has had a dose of laudanum, and I hope she is asleep by now. Come tomorrow morning—not too early—a night's sleep should have improved her.'

He felt baffled and frustrated. Tomorrow morning! That was an age away. He could not go back to Queen Square yet. He would go to the Rooms, and then finish the night in Hell.

All day Kate had waited for Harry to come. She grew more and more anxious, and finally gave up hope. His mother must have convinced him that she was a thoroughly bad wife and mother. She would not see him again. She refused to give way to tears; with stubborn determination she went, not to bed, but to Hell, earlier than usual, thus forcing Sophia to lie to cover up her absence from Miles's Buildings.

She began to make arrangements with Hobley to close the club and pay off the 'devils'. Tomorrow would be the last night. She would not give in to Carbern—she must defy him—but somehow she must see Harry first and tell him the truth. If he had to learn that she was Madam Satan, he had best learn it from her lips, in any case it would end her marriage once and for all. The future now looked utterly black and void; how she would live she did not know, but surely there was nothing more that could happen now?

She was wrong: Fate had yet another trick to play on her.

The men came on from the Assembly Rooms; the club began to fill. Carbern arrived with his clique, and Kate's heart sank to see that they were followed soon after by Harry. She prayed that Carbern would not push her into any kind of scene that evening. Then another bad omen —Sir Claude Vernett came teetering in, leaning on the arm of Richard Stukely.

Several times she saw Carbern glancing at her, and realised he could hardly contain his impatience. She tried to avoid him, but dared not make this obvious, and before long he cornered her.

'Well, Madam Satan, have you come to a decision?' he muttered.

'You are an hour or two early, Lord Carbern.'

'Don't trifle with me! A couple of hours makes no difference! Well, will you or will you not give me what I ask?'

She took a deep breath. 'No, I will not.'

He swore foully in a vicious undertone, his eyes blazing.

'Then you must take the consequences. When I've finished, you'll be in the gutter, you'll be begging me to take you.'

For a moment he glared down at her, his face livid, his eyes narrowed, his mouth twisted in a bitter sneer. She had the sudden fear that he was going to snatch off her hood, and she put her hand to her throat, holding the base of the hood against her.

'No, not yet—but when I choose,' he said, and turned on his heel, shouting, 'Claude, is there room for me at your table?'

Kate tried to behave normally, moving about the room, checking on one table and then another, but she was haunted by Carbern's threat, and also uncomfortably aware of the presence of the other two men who had influenced her life. Harry, characteristically, was playing piquet with quiet concentration. This was a game in which intelligence was important, it relied least of all games on chance. Carbern was playing faro, and having his usual good luck. It was uncanny; when other players were consistently losing and enriching the bank, he would go on winning.

Stukely could not seem to settle, but went from table to table. He started with bassett, but after a while deserted the cards for dice and played hazard; then he went back to cards again. He played piquet against old Lord Cambrell and beat him. The young men, seeing him cock-a-hoop, and considering such a display as a sign of a lack of breeding, began slyly to bait him, suggesting he should find an opponent more worthy of him. In no time at all he had been manoeuvred into playing against Carbern.

Stukely was not a fool; he was a good player, though not as clever as he thought himself to be. Play went back and forth for a while, neither winning nor losing extravagantly. Then Carbern's luck temporarily deserted him: he was getting poor cards, and Stukely was winning. Unperturbed, Carbern went on playing. Stukely, who had already drunk a fair amount, called for more wine. His usually ruddy face was flushed more deeply, he began to exult noisily over his excellent play.

'Egad, man, you're not a town crier,' Carbern remarked. 'More stakes and less noise would suit me. Who introduced this fellow? Claude? You're a nincompoop!'

'You want to raise the odds again?' Stukely cried. 'I've got your measure! You'll come to grief!'

'I'll match anything you wager.'

The bets were laid and play continued. Whether it was through over-confidence, change of luck, or the wine —or all three—Stukely began to lose his grip of the game, and the winning streak deserted him. Carbern still looked calm and supercilious, but his eyes had begun to show that spark of intensity which betrayed that gambling fever was mounting. Stukely was looking illtempered. As loss succeeded loss, his face darkened, he renewed his stakes with a bad grace. He dealt, played, and lost again. Now it was Carbern's deal. Kate was at another table, and as a group of onlookers had collected to watch Stukely and Carbern, she could not see what happened, but she heard Stukely raise a shout and call Carbern a cheat.

She rose swiftly and went over to them. If she did not smooth this over, there would be trouble. The bystanders parted for her, and she saw Hobley moving over from the other side of the room. She hoped she would not have need of him.

'Gentlemen, let us have no quarrel. The hand shall be invalid.'

'Why, madam, that I cannot accept,' Carbern said coldly. 'The fellow called me a cheat. I never cheat. For anyone to cheat with this opponent would be ludicrously unnecessary. The man's a fool—and a knave as well, it seems.'

Stukely stood up, overturning his chair. 'I said you cheated, you jackanapes, and I repeat it! You . . .'

'Wait!' said Kate crisply. 'There were plenty of people watching. Did anyone see anything amiss?'

There were cries of 'No! Nothing!' and a number of remarks uncomplimentary to Stukely.

'There are no witnesses to agree with you, sir. You will kindly retract that accusation.'

'Retract! I'll see him in hell first!'

'You are seeing me in Hell now,' retorted Carbern blandly. 'I have been more than patient with you. Retract, or give me satisfaction.'

'My lord, duelling is against the law,' Kate protested.

'But it is still practised,' said Carbern. 'At times like this, a man must defend his reputation. Well, sir?'

'I'll give you satisfaction!' Stukely ground out. 'I'll satisfy you with a dose of lead.'

A roar of laughter went up.

'Faith, you must consider yourself a good shot!' Sir Augustus shouted.

Stukely glared at him. 'I'm a damn good shot, sir! I've killed more game than you've emptied pint pots!'

Carbern stifled a yawn. 'Kill all the game you like. I have killed men, and shall shortly kill you. Gussie, will you be my second? The choice of weapons is yours, sir.'

'Pistols, of course. Will someone serve me as second?'

This had gone too far, Kate thought. 'Gentlemen, for the sake of the club, I must ask you not to duel.'

Carbern shook his head. 'The matter is settled, madam. All we need now is to fix time and place.'

'As soon as you choose. This morning, when it's light enough,' Stukely growled. 'Kingsmead fields, I suppose.'

Sir Claude was pressed as a most unwilling second to Stukely, so everything was in hand.

'We have plenty of time to sober up,' said Carbern. 'And to take a few more turns at faro.'

Not to be outdone, Stukely intimated that he wished to continue to play, but now, no one would join his table.

'What a lily-livered lot you are!' he shouted. 'Are you afraid to lose, or afraid of another duel? I'll take on any number of you dainty lads!'

Still no one would play with him, and he began to look dangerously angry. Kate thought: He is my enemy. Win or lose, I deserve a bout with him.

'Since you are in need of an opponent, sir, will you play with me? I will give you a game of piquet,' she offered.

He looked surprised; he paused, then laughed. 'Damme, I've never played piquet with a woman before.'

'If you want a game, sir, you must do so now.'

'Very well.'

They seated themselves; a devil laid a short pack of cards between them, and scoring-boards to the side.

'Satisfy yourself as to the cards, sir,' said Kate.

He flipped quickly through them, looking and counting; thirty-two, the correct number. They cut for choice of deal; Stukely won, and gave the deal to Kate, which meant he had the advantage for the partie of six deals. They settled to bet on each deal, and to raise the stakes if they chose. Kate dealt, twelve cards each, in pairs, the remaining eight between them, face down, and play began with Stukely making his exchange.

Kate felt she was his match, but he had the advantage and better cards, and she lost the first game, and with it her first stake, the scores being recorded towards the result of the whole partie. Now it was Stukely's deal. Her concentration was not complete, she was somewhat hampered by the knowledge that a quarrel in her club had provoked a duel, and by the fact that she had never before played for high stakes. She did not approve of high play, it was profligate, unnecessarily risky. Some strange impulse of revenge had pushed her into taking Stukely on, and now she must go through with it.

She lost again, and her mood changed.

No longer was she Kate Breedon, gambling high against her principles, but Madam Satan, the equal at cards of any man there, and she would prove it. Stukely might be—was—a shrewd player, but he had not her brain, and his acuteness was beginning to be dulled by drink and the anticipation of what the dawn might bring; she would play as high as he chose, and beat him.

He had doubled and redoubled the stakes, and was now noisily confident. 'You shouldn't have taken me on, Madam Satan! I'll have your money—and I'll win Hell off you before morning!'

'We shall see, sir. We have not finished yet.'

They went on playing. Kate won, and won again. The situation was changing, the scores were evening up.

There had been a crowd round the table at the start; now the players sat within a circle of men astride chairs they had pulled over from other tables, and behind them other men were standing. Play had ceased in the rest of the room.

A woman might play a man at piquet in a private house, when all she would lose would be the points scored against her; but for a woman to gamble against a man for high stakes, and at a game of skill, was most unusual. But this was a most unusual woman: she had a cool head, a clear brain, a quick wit—and a black hood which concealed her looks, her thoughts, her emotions from them.

The room was hot, the air thick with the smell of candlewax, tobacco-smoke and sweat. Kate longed to remove her hood, for it added to her discomfort. But beside concealing her identity it was a defence. It gave her an air of mystery, it set her apart, it turned her from a mere woman into a strange, almost mystic figure, it allowed her to dominate and made the men defer to her. She raised a glass of wine to the mouth-slit of her hood and took a sip, just enough to moisten her mouth, and play resumed.

Stukely lost again—now he was in deep, and could hardly control his temper. They finished the second partie.

'Damme if you haven't cleaned me out! What a cursed run of luck! I've nothing more to stake with in ready money—if I had, my luck would turn, I'd get it back.'

'Don't worry, you won't need it tomorrow!' someone shouted.

With a snarl, he turned on them. 'I'll be back tomorrow evening, when you're burying your friend! God's blood, I'd like to go on playing!'

Suddenly Kate felt all her hatred for him rising within her, and she heard herself saying, as coolly as you please, 'Would you, sir? Then there is a way. I'll double and redouble my last stake—and you can wager some of your property against it, on one more partie—we have plenty of witnesses to the agreement.'

'Egad, that's an idea! Now, what shall I wager?'

'I shall tell you. I believe you have a little manor —Walton—no, Walcotte, I think? I will accept that as stake—house and contents, and the manor lands. If you win the partie you'll have a good bargain, for I understand it's run down, and not worth much.'

'Done!' said Stukely. 'We'll play your redouble against Walcotte.'

He was plainly too deep in the game to wonder how she knew that Walcotte belonged to him.

It was Kate's deal again, so he had the advantage. Her cards, even when she had exchanged, were poor; he called a point of five.

'Good,' she responded—her point was three.

'A sequence of five.'

'Good.'

'A set of four.'

'Good.'

She could not even equal any of his calls.

His score was mounting; he had a good score before they started trick play, and with his cards there was no way she could catch him in that game. She consoled herself that the next lead was hers.

This game went better for her, but she still could not reach his score. He began to exult, crowing that his luck had changed. Two more games, and the play went back and forth, neither having outstanding luck, and both playing well. Stukely was not as affected by the wine as she had hoped. He still had the better score, though his advantage was not great.

In the fifth game he was cock-a-hoop, saying he had never been beaten by a woman at anything, and would not start now. She ignored his gibes; she could not afford to let him upset her concentration. Her cards were quite good, but the change and draw did not improve them and she had to fight for each point, especially as Stukely declared 'carte blanche'—a bonus of ten. She told herself it would not be a matter of life or death if she lost, but she knew she could not afford to do so, and besides, her heart was set on beating him. At the end of the fifth game he was still ahead.

For the last game it was his deal, and therefore her advantage. Whatever her cards, she must play an attacking game. She picked them up, and saw they were good. An exchange would be a gamble, yet she took it, exchanging three. To her delight they improved her hand. He could not equal any of her calls; what was more, she reached thirty before he scored, so she repiqued. The sixty points it gave her could be crucial. Stukely's look darkened, and he swore. She checked her mounting excitement, and they played their tricks. Stukely stood no chance against her; coolly she played her last card, and totalled all the tricks and then the score for all six games. She had won the partie.

Suddenly she felt exhausted, but she would not let herself relax. Stukely leaned back in his chair, staring, incredulous; he could not believe he had been defeated, that he had lost so much money, and Walcotte as well. Around them men were laughing and cheering, while in the background Harry Breedon stood, a host of thoughts, which were only now making a clear pattern, hidden behind an impassive face.

Kate beckoned to Hobley.

'Devil One, pen, ink and paper, if you please.'

A buzz of talk had broken out after the cheering which had ended the fascinated silence. Someone said, 'Well done, Madam Satan! You're a player to be reckoned with!' Carbern remarked, 'What does Madam Satan want with a run-down manor, I wonder?'

'Nothing, sir,' she retorted swiftly. 'It was convenient, that is all.'

She ignored the warning shiver running up her spine, and signed to Hobley to give the writing materials to Stukely.

'Now, sir, you will write. "I, Richard Stukely"—that is your name, I believe?—"do hereby assign the Manor of Walcotte in the county of Somerset, its contents and manor lands, to—"'

The silence was complete. Everyone waited for the name which would reveal her identity.

'Leave a space there, sir, and continue.'

There were shouts of 'Tell us, Madam Satan!' and 'The name! The name!' but she took no notice. Stukely, in a foul temper, wrote a wretched hand, pressing and scratching so that the quill squeaked and spluttered, but finally he came to an end.

'You will sign it, sir, and we will have your signature witnessed. But first, to fill that space.'

Everyone was quiet again. They waited.

'I have been thinking,' she said coldly. 'A manor is no use to Madam Satan. Fill in the name of the woman from whom you filched it, Katharine Walcotte.'

'I did not filch . . .' he began, but she interrupted him.

'No? Well, it does not matter. *Write*—"to Katharine Walcotte, now Katharine Breedon, Viscountess Stonebridge." Sign it.'

'What does it matter to me?' he muttered, and wrote the name, adding an awkward, sprawling signature. The two men nearest him put their names as witnesses, Hobley dusted the paper with pounce, shook off the powder and handed the paper to Kate.

She read it through carefully, then folded it, and lifting the edge of her hood, put the paper in the bosom of her gown.

Stukely got unsteadily to his feet. 'Damn you all!' he shouted. 'I'm off—I've better things to do than stay here!'

There was a storm of shouts and jeers.

'Make your will!'

'Ay—sober up—you couldn't hit a barn-door now, much less Clever Carbern!'

'Say your prayers, if you know any!'

Pushing through the men, knocking over chairs, Stukely stormed out of the room. Carbern, who had been watching with a cynical smile, now spoke, and his drawling voice cut through the talk of the other men.

'Gentlemen, has it not occurred to you to wonder why Madam Satan should be so generous to a lady who is surely not in need of a poor little property?'

Someone murmured, 'That is her affair', and Carbern turned on him swiftly. Kate held her breath.

'But it will be interesting to all. For I can tell you.'

Kate's throat tightened in nervous dread. Carbern looked around at his audience.

'It is very simple,' he went on. 'It is because Madam Satan and Viscountess Stonebridge are one and the same person.'

There were roars of incredulous laughter, shouts of 'Impossible!' 'Prove it!' 'A fine tale!' and a burst of excited speculation. Now that it had come, it was almost a relief. At least she had salvaged something; she could live in retirement at Walcotte, and spend her time running the estate.

By now the men had all turned to look at Harry. A derisive smile was on his lips, and the room became quiet after the initial uproar as the men waited for his response. He gave a brief, contemptuous laugh. Katharine could not move; she could hardly breathe. If only she could delay disclosure, to save Harry's face in front of all these men.

At last he spoke. 'Damme, Carbern, you are making a fool of yourself. Does anyone think I do not know my own wife?'

A slight flush crept into Carbern's face, his eyes narrowed and his mouth set in an angry line.

'Many men do not, and you have been long away. The matter is easily proved. Madam Satan can settle it at once by removing her hood.'

At this Kate found her wits and her voice. She would give Carbern a run for his money.

'And why should I, my lord? I consider the lady has a right to her own property, and I am prepared to make her a present of it. But I do not see that my goodwill obliges me to reveal what I choose to keep secret.'

Carbern leaned forward and stared at her. 'That's a pretty excuse, but it won't wash. I say you are Lady Kate—*disprove it if you can!*'

'I do not choose. If the lady does not like your suggestion, then she must fend for herself.'

Harry's voice broke in, the words steady, unhurried, but with a note of warning.

'You are very free with my wife's name, Carbern. Madam Satan runs a good, clean club, and I respect her for it, but to couple her name with my wife's is nonsense, and nonsense to which I object. And I, of all men, should know the truth.'

The atmosphere in the room was tense. Now no one was looking at her. This had suddenly become an issue between the two men, and it was anyone's guess how it would turn out. Carbern cast one long glance at Kate's still figure, then turned back to Harry with an insolent smile.

'You say it is nonsense. I say it is true. You say you should know, but time tells, Stonebridge. I am more intimate with your wife than you realise.'

There was a quick gasp from the listening men. Harry's eyes blazed, and his face was livid. He shouldered aside the men nearest to Carbern, stood for a moment, and then gave him a swift hard blow across the face.

'You are a damned, disreputable liar, and you will take back your words or give me satisfaction!'

Carbern, one cheek flaming from the blow, stared at Harry with total malevolence.

'I take nothing back. You can have satisfaction! Take your turn behind that other fool, Stukely!'

Kate thought: If I show them who I am, perhaps Harry will not have cause to fight. Then she remembered Carbern's words—'I am more intimate with your wife than you realise . . .' and knew, regardless of everything else, it was an insult that Harry would never let pass.

'Very well. This morning.'

Kate tried to fight off the feeling of horror which engulfed her.

'*Not* this morning,' Sir Augustus objected. 'It's hard enough to settle one duel nowadays. If we hang around after the first, we'll all be taken.'

There was a general murmur of agreement.

'Very well,' said Carbern grudgingly. 'I'll fight Stukely

this morning and Stonebridge the morning after.'

'If you survive,' said Harry coolly.

'Don't think you'll get off so lightly! I'll survive!'

Now Carbern's closest friends were urging him to leave, to break for the few short hours before dawn, when he would go to Kingsmead fields. He came to Kate and bowed elaborately in farewell.

'Good night, Madam Satan. That little matter between us will be settled before long.'

She did not answer, but stood still and silent as Carbern and a cluster of friends went through the door.

The excitement was over, but the club was not empty. The dedicated gamblers returned to the tables; they would not be satisfied until the money ran out or they were overcome by exhaustion. With a sudden shock, Kate realised that Harry had not left.

He made no move to speak to her, but called for some cold meat and a bottle of wine. Kate's nerves were in tatters. What had she done for Fate to treat her so? Or was it all her fault that the man she loved was now probably only a day away from death? She had thought she could never be so vicious as to hope for a man's life to be ended, and she knew she hated Stukely, but now she found herself wishing that he would kill Carbern. That was the only way for Harry to be kept out of danger. But there was little chance of that. Carbern had the reputation of a deadly duellist, with at least three men buried with his bullets in them. He always shot to kill. He would shoot Stukely down, then calmly turn and make arrangements to meet Harry with the same intention.

Harry—that he should survive so much, and die like that, and for her good name. She could not bear the thought. But she would have to bear it till the end of her days. That would be the penalty of her pride and folly.

She was still Madam Satan. Her professional skill made her aware of something out of the ordinary. She noticed that one of the 'devils' was speaking to Hobley, not in the quiet calm manner she demanded, but with an insistence made more marked by urgent gestures. As she watched, Hobley motioned him into silence and came over to her.

'Madam—bad news,' he said crisply. 'A friend of Sir Claude's, spending the evening with the magistrate, has sent to tell him to leave the club now.'

'He has already left. But why?'

'That's it, madam. The magistrate has been told about Hell, and is assembling constables to raid us, and arrest as many of us as they can.'

The last blow, she thought. But she would go down fighting. She clapped her hands, and raised her voice so that all in the room should hear her.

'Gentlemen, I advise you to leave at once. I have been warned that officers of the law are about to raid us. Collect your belongings and go. Devils, come to me for orders.'

There was a burst of excited talk as the men picked up coats, wigs, cravats, snuff-boxes, stake-money, all their impedimenta, and without stopping to dress, hurried and bustled to the door. While they clattered out, her devils crowded around her.

'We close a day early,' she said drily. 'You have been paid up, but here's a sovereign more for each man to help clear this room as fast as possible. When it's packed up, down the back stairs and away with you!—And thank you all!'

She stood for a moment, watching the scurry of movement. Someone came up to her. It was Harry.

Harry! He had not left! But, thank heaven, she was still wearing her hood.

'You must go, sir,' she said.

'Don't be a fool, Kate. I must see you out of here. Have you any incriminating papers?'

He knew! Shock struck her like a blow, but there was no time to think of anything but Hell, and she rallied herself.

'Yes,' she answered swiftly. 'A list of members, and my accounts.'

'Get them. Burn them. Where are they?'

'Downstairs.'

As she hurried to the door, he was behind her. Picking up her skirts she fled through the anteroom, down the stairs and into the room off the hallway. She opened a desk and pulled out a ledger and some papers.

'That's all? You've a fire in the kitchen?' Harry asked.

'Yes.'

'Burn them there. There's not much, thank God.'

He almost pushed her out of the room, and she ran through the door at the back of the hall and down the stairs to the basement kitchen. In there, the cook and kitchen-boy seemed unaware of what was going on.

As Kate went to the fire, she called, 'We're going to be raided. Put the food in the larder, make the kitchen look fairly clear, and be off!'

Startled, they glanced at each other and then did as she said. Soon there was a clatter of feet on the stairs. The devils rushed down, and seizing such belongings as they had left in the basement passage they made a swift exit, some up the area steps, and some, joined by the cook and kitchen-boy, by the garden door out into the greying dark.

Harry came into the kitchen with Hobley behind him

as Kate was tearing out the last pages and pushing them into the fire.

'It's clear enough upstairs,' said Harry. 'Ready, Kate? We'll leave.'

'Come, then,' she answered, motioning to Hobley.

'Not me, m'lady. His lordship reckons it's best if I stay. I'll be a sleepy caretaker who's been entertaining his friends on the sly while the owner's away.'

'Are you sure? When they come, they'll question you . . .'

'I know what to say.'

'They'll ask who the owner is.'

Harry's voice was crisp and decisive. 'Viscount Stonebridge, of course. Now, Kate, come at once.'

Hobley was already holding her cloak for her.

'Thank you, John.'

She let Harry bundle her out, and heard Hobley lock the back door behind them.

It was still very dark, with only a faint greyness presaging the dawn as they stumbled down the garden path. Harry muttered a curse as he fumbled for the latch of the door at the end. Then he found it, pulled the door open and they slipped through. As they did so, they heard hurried footsteps at the end of the path where it opened into George Street.

Harry's hand came up and snatched the hood from her head. He pushed it into one of the deep pockets of his coat and led her quickly across the road. Men were running down the front of the houses in Miles' Buildings, though they were as yet invisible. Suddenly he took her in his arms and kissed her, long, passionately, holding her close, and at the same time pulling the hood of her cloak over her head. The kiss went on, raising a new tumult within her, making the fear and urgency of the last quarter of an hour recede into near-unreality. This, for now, was all that mattered. She gave herself up to his kiss, lips parting in total surrender.

A rough voice cut into the wonder of it.

'Hey, who are you?'

Harry, still holding her hood against her head so that her face was shadowed, raised his head and answered brusquely and with aristocratic authority, 'What the devil d'ye mean? Don't interrupt a gentleman in his amusements! Get about your business, if you have any!'

The tone of the strange voice changed at one. 'Beg pardon, sir—my mistake.'

He moved away. Another voice said gruffly, 'This is the door we want.'

Harry held her close again, his lips pressed to her cheek, until they heard the men—three or four of them, she guessed—go through the garden door opposite and stumble up the path. Then he let her go and led her to her own front door.

'Your key, Kate.'

Another moment, and they were inside the dark hall of the little house in Miles's Buildings.

CHAPTER
TEN

So MANY thoughts and questions were whirling in Kate's mind that she could not give voice to one of them. In a daze she moved mechanically through the dark hall to where a single candle burned, and began to light from it the double branch which stood ready for her beside it. She turned back to Harry.

'There's so much to say, my love . . .'

'Not now,' he answered, and took her in his arms again. 'What does it all matter? *This* is what counts.'

Once again he kissed her; love and longing rose within her, her pulses quickened, her body weakened. With his mouth still on hers he drew the cloak from her shoulders and it fell to the floor. His hands caressed her.

'I've been a blind fool,' he muttered, laying his cheek against hers. 'I'll try to make amends. But for me, only one thing matters. Do you love me, Kate? God knows there's no reason why you should.'

'Oh, Harry, with all my heart—and have done, for a long while.'

'And you—you crept into my heart—all your infuriating ways, your rebellions . . .'

'I am not infuriating!'

His reply was to kiss her repeatedly, softly, seductively, his lips playing with hers, while his hands strayed over the curves of her body.

'Of course you are, my darling,' he whispered. 'I am in a fury now—maddened by the need for you, loving every inch of you. Everything that makes you different from all the others, the humdrum women, makes me adore you all the more. Until I kissed you out there in the street I was unsure of you—but now—tell me you need me, as I need you!'

With something between a laugh and a sob she answered, 'I've been waiting so long to hear you say that. Harry, dearest, you are the only man for me!'

'Sweetheart . . . Then why are we standing in this draughty hall?'

He picked up the candlestick.

'Come, Kate, show me which is your room. I have no wish to walk in upon Sophia.'

'Are you asking to stay here for the rest of the night?' she murmured.

'No, I am insisting. Just for once, you are going to let me have my own way, without an argument.'

With an arm round her waist, he was already urging her up the stairs.

'That's a dangerous precedent,' she whispered, trying not to sound delighted.

She laid her hand upon the door; he turned the knob and they slipped inside. He closed the door, set down the candle, and caught her in his arms again.

'You're mine!' he said with fierce intensity. 'By God, I should never have left you!'

Forget tomorrow, she said to herself. Tonight—this hour—this moment—I belong to Harry as never before, and he to me. 'You never left my heart!'

There was no more need for words. This was surrender, and she gloried in it.

*   *   *

Richard Stukely's death caused more of a sensation than anything in his life. Duels, now illegal, were rare enough to raise a stir, particularly when they were fatal, and the surgeon who had attended the dying man had said there certainly had been a duel, though by the time he reached the scene all the other participants had disappeared. Stukely had been too far gone to name his opponent, even had he wished to do so. There were plenty of opinions concerning the man's identity, but no proof. The scandal of the duel quite overshadowed the raid on a high-class gambling house, which, since it was unsuccessful and totally inconclusive, had no gossip value.

Kate, having put everything but the perfect happiness of the moment out of her thoughts, had slept more soundly than she had done for months, and woke to find Harry already up and dressed.

He stooped over the bed and kissed her.

'I must leave you for now, dearest. I have much to do today. I'll come back here this afternoon and then we can talk.'

She flung her arms round his neck.

'Don't go now, Harry—there are things I must ask you . . .'

'Yes, Kate, but later. It's not only broad daylight, but the day is advanced, and lawyers take their time.'

'*Lawyers!*'

The full horror of it flashed on her. He had to face a duel in the coming dawn. He was going to make his will, for by this time tomorrow he might be dead.

'Don't look so stricken, Kate. One takes precautions —and then probably they are not needed.'

He unclasped her hands from his neck and kissed her again. 'Till this afternoon.'

It was while Kate was trying to eat some breakfast, with Sophia, who had risen much earlier, sharing her coffee, that Mrs Partridge came in with the news of Stukely's death.

'The butcher-boy told the cook, but it's true enough,' she said. 'Most people think it was my lord Carbern, but no one can prove it.'

Kate said nothing. What news would the butcher-boy be retailing tomorrow? She felt physically sick; mentally helpless and hopeless.

During the morning, she told Sophia and Mrs Partridge what had happened in Hell the night before. They tried to console her.

'Perhaps someone will stop the duel,' said Sophia hopefully.

'What use would that be?' Kate replied. 'It would only postpone it—Carbern would find some other time and place.'

The hours dragged on. She tried to eat to please Sophia, but every morsel had to be forced down, and her stomach rebelled. At Sophia's insistence she took a little brandy, and for a while felt physically somewhat better.

At last Harry returned. 'Now we can talk,' he said. 'Don't go, Sophia. You are Kate's friend, and know all our business.'

He told them briefly of the scene he had had with his parents.

'I think I made them both ashamed of themselves. My mother, of course, does not change easily. My father is not ill-intentioned, Kate, he is weak, and in the past has given in to my mother for the sake of peace. But he'll keep a restraining hand on her from now on. He likes you; in fact, he admires your courage. If you return, you will have your proper place in their house, with no interference in the nursery. But I have told them we may set up a separate establishment when we see our future more clearly.'

You mean, if you survive, Kate thought.

'I have made my arrangements,' Harry went on calmly. 'Whatever happens, you are provided for and will not suffer.'

Kate looked at him in horror. He meant he had made his will—the best provision he could in case of his death.

'Not *suffer!* Without you, Harry, I should suffer always, for the duel is *my* fault—without me it would never have . . .'

'Now, Kate! You mustn't feel like that. It was my choice.'

He put his arm round her. She tried to think of something else, and for a moment she succeeded.

'Harry, when did you know I was Madam Satan?'

'Long before Carbern revealed it. There is no one like you. It would take more than a hood to hide you from me.'

'And weren't you shocked—disgusted, even?'

'Shocked, yes. But when I knew what you had been through, I could see what had caused you to take that role upon yourself. I couldn't blame you.'

'I never thought you would understand.'

'All the same, I don't want it to be public knowledge. We now stand a chance of it remaining a somewhat embarrassing rumour.'

Sophia's gentle voice broke in. 'I cannot help wondering why the magistrate suddenly decided to raid the club.'

'*Why?*' Harry repeated. 'Didn't either of you guess?'

'Do you know?' asked Kate.

'It's plain enough to me,' he retorted. 'Stukely informed on you. To him it was a good move. If the raid had been successful, both Carbern and I would have been detained. We'd be released on bail, but there'd be some scandal, with Carbern probably under enough surveillance to make his duel with Stukely most unwise. As for you—he wouldn't forgive Madam Satan for beating him at cards, and the possession of paper giving the ownership of Walcotte would convict the woman who had it on her person as proprietress of Hell. She would pay for it, being tried and sentenced.'

'He hated me, of course. And you, I suppose.'

'He gave me proof of it. Well, he's struck his last blow.'

'But now—there is still Carbern.'

'I shall deal with him, and blast out his filthy imputations.'

'But why duel, Harry?' she cried. 'What I know, and you believe, is all that matters. Let society think what they choose! I want you alive. What use is my good name to me without you?'

'Kate, that's a woman's point of view,' said Harry gently. 'You must allow me mine. I couldn't live with myself if I let Carbern speak his filthy lies unchecked.'

'But he is a duellist, and you are not! He has an unfair advantage—and in any case, a duel proves nothing, except your willingness to risk your life. Are you going to chance making me a widow, and Edward an orphan, just to satisfy your pride?'

'Yes, Kate.'

That evening, Kate went with Harry to Queen Square. Lady Cecily received her with reserved politeness, but Lord Embercombe, as soon as he saw there was no rancour in Kate's attitude, was jovial and welcoming. His temperament was such that it was easy for him to forget the past, particularly if he had been at fault. Kate's one real concern was for Edward. He was such a solemn little boy at times that she was not sure whether he recognised her, but he accepted her, and they were soon playing together.

Harry went back with her to Miles's Buildings.

'I feel more alone with you in your little house,' he said. 'Besides, to be brutally honest, it would be difficult for me to leave Queen Square before dawn without causing a stir. I prefer my parents to know nothing about the duel until it is over.'

Over, one way or the other, thought Kate. Only a miracle could save it from the most lamentable conclusion. But she was not going to waste Harry's last hours in weeping and regrets. If they had so little time, they must fill it with happiness. They knew now that they loved each other more deeply than they had ever done, and the expression of that love was an ecstasy that left no room for past doubts and misunderstandings.

As they lay in each other's arms, Harry murmured, 'Whatever happens, Kate, I have no regrets, believe me. I've cheated death on many occasions, and if my time has come now, I know I've been spared long enough to be truly happy. Not many men can say that.'

She could not answer, so she closed his mouth with a kiss.

Dawn broke on a chill autumn morning. Kate wanted to leave with Harry, but he would not hear of it.

'It's no place for you, love.'

As soon as he had gone, she got up and dressed as quickly as she could. There was no way in which he could stop her from following him. He had left on horseback; the groom who had saddled up for him was dropping back into slumber when Kate reached the mews and roused him to harness up the little chaise. To save time, she helped him, though every strap and buckle seemed stiff and refractory to her shaking fingers. When it was done, she mounted and took the reins herself. She wanted to go alone.

She prayed she would not be too late. It would be impossible to prevent the duel, but she must be with Harry at the last moment. The streets were empty. The little carriage woke a hundred echoes as it spun and clattered over the cobbles through the town, down Southgate Street and towards the bridge.

Over Kingsmead fields the mist lay in swirls, like fine white chiffon on the green silk of the grass, drifting and shifting as the men walked through. The sun was low and faint, the air cool and damp. The men had left their horses at some little distance, moving on to a space clear of bushes and undergrowth. There were only five of them; the duellists, their seconds, and the umpire. Even the customary surgeon in charge had been dispensed with, since they did not know one they could trust.

'After yesterday, we can't be too careful,' Carbern had said. 'We don't want our plans leaked out in advance.'

'I agree,' said Harry, and added ironically, 'Don't worry. If I bring you down, I'll give you my professional services.'

'Damn your decency, I believe you would,' was the reply.

But now they were in deadly earnest.

The place was chosen, the case of duelling pistols proffered and accepted. Both men buttoned up their coats in order to reduce the target a white shirt-front would give, and the umpire stationed them in position. He gave his final instructions, then began counting. As he counted, the two men paced away. There was no sound in the damp, chilly air except the mounting numbers.

'Four—five—six—seven . . .'

Suddenly there was movement. A man leapt out from behind some bushes and began to run towards them, shouting, while in the distance, other figures appeared.

'In the name of the law, throw down your pistols!'

Harry stopped, turned, and obeyed. Carbern too swung round, but he raised his pistol, aiming it at Harry's heart. The man who had shouted kept running towards him. Suddenly Carbern seemed to change his mind—moved—and then fired.

The running man fell with a cry. Without a pause, Carbern took to his heels and fled swiftly to where the horses were tethered. Now the other men were close, but he leapt to the saddle and charged off into the thinning mist. From between the other pursuers came a slight figure, hampered by long skirts that dragged through the wet grass. As the duelling team was surrounded, she broke through and flung herself into Harry's arms.

Later, in the house in Miles's Buildings, information and opinions were being exchanged between Kate, Harry and the two Spenlows.

'Why did they arrest you, Harry? You had done nothing,' said Kate.

'No, but I was obviously about to take part in a duel. Why worry? I am released on bail. Nothing will come of it.'

'But why were they lying in wait? How did they know? The duel was a secret between the members of the club, none of whom would have told the magistrate's men.'

'It was the hand of Providence,' said Sophia.

Kate looked at her closely. 'Sophia, you're not usually quite so prim. What do you know?'

'Nothing . . . How could I?'

Herbert Spenlow shifted in his chair. 'Faith, I had better confess. I did it.'

'*You?*' exclaimed Kate.

'Yes. I'm not such a fool as I used to be. I couldn't stand the thought of Carbern shooting Stonebridge down.'

'He fully intended to,' said Kate, looking at Harry. 'When the constable interrupted . . .'

'Yes. He dearly wanted me dead. Then he changed his mind and shot the constable instead. He was the immediate danger.'

'He's not dead?'

'He's recovering. Why did Carbern do it? Because he feared arrest. For all he knew, Stukely's death was being laid at his door. As it happened, by shooting an officer of the law he made sure a warrant was issued. What is more, not only the constable but some of the other men were near enough to identify him.'

'Will they catch him?'

'I doubt it,' Harry replied. 'He'll make for the coast and slip across to France in a fishing-boat. But it will be years before he dares to show his face in England again—if ever.'

Thank God, thought Kate. We're free of him at last.

'One other thing,' said Spenlow, a trifle uneasily. 'You may not like this—but I did it for the best . . .'

'What, another confession?' said Harry.

'Yes. Afterwards, in the coffee-house, some of the men were talking—praising you, Harry, for defending Kate's honour when no one could be quite sure . . . no one thought that Kate had ever been intimate with Carbern, everyone knows her too well. But some agreed it was possible that Kate might have been Madam Satan.'

'It doesn't matter,' said Harry easily. 'They will never know. That woman has quite disappeared.'

'But they had heard that the house in Gay Street was said to be owned by Viscount Stonebridge. In your absence, they said, Kate could well have been using it.'

'It's of no consequence.'

'It could make things difficult for Kate in the future. And I owe Kate a good turn for all she has done for Sophia. So I said I knew who Madam Satan was.'

'The devil you did! I hope you did not say it was Sophia! They'd never have believed that.'

'I'm serious, Stonebridge. I said she was a woman who had once done you a favour, and this was your way of returning it. They were very ready to believe it! But as to the favour . . .'

'You did not specify it, I trust?' Harry asked coolly.

'I thought it better not.'

'Excellent,' said Harry. 'That will give them plenty to gossip about.'

Kate turned to Spenlow. 'I don't know how to thank you,' she said simply. 'I feel ashamed. I haven't been very nice to you recently—and now you do all this for me . . .'

'I deserved your disapproval,' he replied. 'And you were good to Sophia when I could do nothing for her because of my folly.'

'I hope you'll both stay here for as long as you wish,' Kate ventured.

'Oh, Kate!' Sophia exclaimed. 'Well, we'll discuss that later. Now, Herbert, it's time we left Kate and Harry.'

With this, Sophia bustled her brother out of the room.

With one hand under Kate's chin, Harry lifted her face towards him. 'Well, it seems you face the future with a heavy burden.'

'Whatever do you mean?'

'Young Spenlow has preserved your reputation at the expense of mine. Can you endure to be married to a man who is thought to be keeping an ex-mistress?'

'Certainly. In Bath that is considered to be quite the style!'

But she could no longer make jokes, knowing what might have been.

'Oh, Harry!' she cried. 'I don't know how I could endure to live without you.'

'Darling, you won't have to. I don't intend to let you go.'

He put his arms about her. 'Come close to me, Kate. I have been so long with only the dream of you.'

This is no dream, thought Kate, as they clung and kissed. It is still a man's world, but Harry's arms are hard and strong around me, his lips are on my lips, his heart is beating on my heart. I am his woman. This is reality, and it is good enough for me.

Rebecca had set herself on course for loneliness and despair. It took a plane crash and a struggle to survive in the wilds of the Canadian Northwest Territories to make her change – and to let her fall in love with the only other survivor, handsome Guy McLaren.

Arctic Rose is her story – and you can read it from the 14th of February for just £2.25.

The story continues with Rebecca's sister, Tamara, available soon.